Kiss It Better

LINDA KAGE

D1714645

Kiss It Better

Copyright © 2013 by Linda Kage

Contact Information : linda@lindakage.com

Publishing History
1ˢᵗ Edition Whispers Publishing, August 2011
2nd Edition Linda Kage, July 2013
Print ISBN: 978-1490471624

Credits
Cover Artist: Viola Estrella Design
Editor: Jessica Damien

Published in the United States of America

DEDICATION

For a wonderful mentor,
Nan D. Arnold
1950-2012

CHAPTER 1

"Damn it." Sophia Eschell fisted her hand and gritted her teeth. "I am *so* through with men."

"What was that, honey?"

With a squeak of alarm, Sophia spun around to find a blue-haired secretary peering up at her through a thick set of grandma glasses. Around them, computer keys click-clacked and copy machines beeped.

From her spot in the walkway between cubicles, Sophia cringed. "Sorry, Myrna. I was just talking to...Sweet mercy, I've started talking to myself." Pressing a hand to her brow, she groaned. "God, he's got me talking to myself." *At work, no less.*

Eyes sparkling with suppressed laughter, Myrna guessed, "Man trouble?"

Sophia snorted. "Jerk trouble's more like it." Plopping onto the edge of Myrna's desk, she gave a long, shoulder-slumping sigh. "Tell me honestly, Myr. Is there something wrong with me?"

"Sweetie, there's nothing wrong with you." Making a tsking sound, Myrna patted her knee. "Tell old Myrna what happened."

"There's this guy," Sophia started, then sniffed. "Gary. I've

1

been seeing him for a few weeks now. He just went through a divorce—at least, he *told* me he'd just gone through a divorce. And since his dad left him when he was ten, I thought he was having these major abandonment issues. I felt awful for him. I spent all my free time with him and even helped him pay his rent last month.

"But then today I stopped by his apartment on my break with some take-out, only to learn that someone else had already brought him food. His wife." She covered her face with both hands, too mortified to meet Myrna's accusing stare. "He wasn't divorced at all. Wasn't even considering it."

"Well, hell. He *was* a jerk."

"You're telling me." Sophia lowered her hands. "The trouble is it's been like this with every guy I've dated lately."

Myrna gasped. "They're all married?"

"No, no, of course not. But they all had some kind of major baggage in their lives. I keep thinking I can help them. But—"

"You've got too kind a heart. That's your problem."

Sophia sighed. "I thought a kind heart was a plus, not a problem."

"Not when you're dating users. And that's exactly what these men sound like." The older woman pointed at her knowingly. "You're a jerk magnet."

Sophia's scowl showed her lack of appreciation for the title. "A jerk magnet? I don't want to be a jerk magnet. Where the hell are all the nice guys? Why can't I attract *them?*"

Myrna chuckled. "Oh, they're a rare and scattered breed, my child. Not many around. And the ones who aren't already taken are usually too intimidated to come out of hiding in fear of being trampled by desperate women seeking nice guys like them."

Pushing to her feet, Sophia smoothed out the wrinkles in her slacks. "Thanks a lot, Myrna. Tell me I only attract users and then say all the good guys are afraid of me. I feel so much better. You're a real pal."

"Well, what about my boss?"

Sophia froze at the suggestion. "Reed?" The very name

made her skin prickle with an odd tingling sensation.

"Yes, Reed. None of you girls ever flirt with him, and for the life of me, I can't figure out why not. The boy's a looker. He's clean-cut and sweet as can be. A real gentleman. If I was thirty years younger, I'd be all over him myself."

"Myrna," Sophia murmured, acting scandalized.

Myrna and her high school sweetheart husband of thirty years had three grandchildren together that she constantly bragged about.

Sophia leaned confidentially closer and winked. "My goodness. Does Reed know you have such a crush on him?"

The secretary flushed. "Well, he ought to." Fanning her heated cheeks, she mumbled, "I bring him my famous home-baked cookies at least once a month."

Sophia threw back her head and let out a crack of laughter.

"Eschell," a strident voice bellowed, making her suck in the chuckle and straighten her back.

"Marcus," she answered. Suddenly dead sober, she forced a tight smile for her bald, pear-shaped supervisor, who lumbered toward her.

"You getting paid to stand around, gossiping with Walker's secretary?"

Sophia checked her watch. "Technically, I'm still on my lunch break."

"Well, *she's* not. Why don't you try working for once?"

She bit her tongue. It took everything she had not to suggest he try growing a personality.

Marcus wouldn't know what work was if it licked him in the face. Ninety percent of her job was finishing *his* duties for him, and she didn't appreciate him making her appear lazy.

He was the lazy one. Grr.

Sucking it up, she nodded and pivoted away. "Yes, sir."

She barely made it two steps before he called again. "Hey, Eschell. While you're here, make yourself useful and drop these by Walker's office, will you?"

Sophia glanced at Walker's opened office door a mere five feet away. Then she transferred an amused, knowing smirk

Marcus's way. *What? Too scared to face the intimidating Walker and deliver them yourself*, she was tempted to ask. Humph. Marcus was such a coward.

Not that there was anything remotely approachable about Thaddeus Reed Walker. The man unsettled her too, but on a purely physical level. He was tall, dark-haired, and utterly awe-inspiring, not to mention so far out of her league, she usually settled for sighing over him from afar.

Myrna had to be insane to suggest she actually show her interest in Reed. Seriously, why would he lower himself to consider dating a peon paper-pusher like her? The man was perfect. Even his clothes knew better than to wrinkle after he'd put in a grueling fifteen-hour day.

He'd been employed by Kendrick Advertising for three years now. And in that time, Mr. Kendrick himself had promoted Reed six times until he was currently the senior accountant, second only to Marcus, who happened to be Kendrick's brother-in-law, which pretty much meant Marcus was paid to show up every day while Reed actually ran the show.

Glaring daggers at Sophia, Marcus snapped, "Just do it. And remind him about the Brunetti case meeting on Monday."

"Yes, sir," Sophia repeated.

She slipped the file from his hand, but couldn't stop her smug grin. She loved it that someone on this floor actually flustered Marcus. But she didn't mind doing his bidding. For a chance to be near Reed Walker, she'd gladly play messenger. Maybe she could get a whiff of his exotic cologne and feel the thrill of his pewter grey eyes momentarily focusing on her. Then she could slink back to her desk and dreamily sigh the rest of the afternoon away.

~ * ~

As a call was patched into the corner office on the sixth floor of Kendrick Advertising, the man at the desk pinched the bridge of his nose. This had to be his tenth call in the past hour.

Since he was about to settle a huge account and was busy reviewing last minute details and checking documents for accuracy, everyone and their dog decided they needed his attention.

He entered a few more figures into his computer with one hand as he picked up the receiver with the other and tucked it between his shoulder and ear. "Walker here."

Reed liked his job. He liked his corner office, and he liked taking on most of the responsibilities of his department. Nothing gave him a bigger rush than meeting each challenge and successfully overcoming it. But sometimes, he wished another unnamed individual could learn to do his own job, giving Reed the occasional break.

"Hey," a familiar voice buzzed in his ear. "I'm going to be running a little late tonight. Some ignorant customer wants his commercial sappier. And he refuses to move the deadline back, so now we've got to bust our asses so he can have more heart in his stupid dog food."

Reed leaned back in his chair and grinned. "Then I'll be sure to keep the chicken warm for you until you get home. Okay, darling?"

"What I meant, *dork*," his roommate Nic muttered, his voice irritated, "is that I'm expecting a call. I've got a date tonight, and I think I gave her our home number instead of my cell. So if she tries to get a hold of me before I make it home, I need you to tell her why I'm tied up and that I'll call as soon as I can."

The mere thought of Nic spending another night out while Reed was stuck home alone—dateless again—did nothing to improve his already pounding head. He pulled open his top desk drawer and began to rummage.

"Why don't you call her and tell her yourself?" He frowned into the crowded tray. Where was his Tylenol?

"I, uh…" Nic hesitated. "I never quite got her number. So…could you get that for me too whenever she calls?"

Reed snorted. "Figures. Okay, whatever. What's this one's name so I can tell the right woman you're going to be late?"

"That's the best part."

Reed could almost see his friend smirking on the other end and rubbing his hands together with relish. "Why? Did you forget her name too?"

"No. That's what I remember. Her name's Toffee. You know, like the candy."

The lucky jerk. Not only did Nic get himself a woman, but he'd found one with a sweet name that probably did all sorts of sweet stuff.

"Toffee, huh? Sounds…tasty." Where was that stupid bottle? He knew it had to be in here—

Ahh. There it was.

In his ear, Nic's voice cooed, "You have no idea just how tasty."

Reed rolled his eyes and pulled the Tylenol free. "Fine. I'll play messenger for you."

A knock made him glance up. The strawberry blonde goddess framed in his open doorway had him shoving the pain reliever back in his drawer and forgetting to breathe. "Just a sec." He covered the mouthpiece and managed to rasp, "What's up?"

The leggy woman wearing tan slacks and a black waist jacket smiled, making his salivary glands work overtime. He licked his lips and swallowed.

As she entered the office, his heart rate doubled. She wasn't the type that walked, but strolled. He knew she didn't intend for her swaying hips to be flirtatious, but they teased him anyway. His throat burned, probably because his mouth, which had been too wet a microsecond ago, suddenly went bone dry, like it usually did whenever he saw her.

He didn't notice the files in her possession until she tapped them against her free hand. "Marcus told me to pass these along to you."

She had a low voice, almost like a smoker's, but he'd bet ten to one she'd never lit up in her life. The rich flavor of it reminded him of a full-bodied wine and always left him a little lightheaded, again, probably because the blood vacated his brain and headed south every time she drew near.

Reed nodded, then cleared his throat. "Just, uh…you can drop it there." He pointed to a wire tray at the corner of his desk.

Watching her set the file down, he slid his gaze up slim fingers to her face. Her exotic almond-shaped, whiskey-colored eyes turned his way.

"And I'm supposed to remind you we've got the Brunetti meeting first thing Monday morning."

His lips spread. "I remember." He had to swallow a sigh when she returned his smile.

"I didn't think you'd forget. Just following orders."

"Well…keep up the good work."

Keep up the good work? Gah! He almost smacked himself. What kind of corny line was that? But she laughed a low, husky trill, and his heartbeat stuttered as the sound moved through him.

"Thanks for taking that off my hands."

"No problem." He watched her turn away.

His mouth fell open when he caught how well her slacks molded to her backside, giving him a brief glimpse of panty line.

God, he loved panty lines.

He waited until she was out of his office before sighing. "No. Thank *you*." He shook his head. "I could die a happy man just ogling those legs."

"Gee, thanks," a voice buzzed in his ear. "I wasn't sure if you'd noticed how much I'd been working out lately."

Reed pulled the phone away from his ear to give it a dirty look. He brought it back. "Not you. Her."

"Who?"

"You know."

There was a pause, and then Nic drawled out one long syllable. "Ohh. Sophia, huh?"

"I don't know what I'm going to do, Nic."

Reed yanked the bottle out of his drawer and flipped off the lid with his thumb. He sprinkled a few tablets into his palm.

"She's driving me insane. I sit by her in all these meetings, and let me tell you, no woman has ever smelled like this. I swear she bathes in some kind of aphrodisiac. You have no idea what it's like, trying to concentrate when her knee is just inches from mine. Then she'll go and cross her legs. And seriously, Nic. These legs are like five miles long. All I can think about is how many times they could wrap around me."

"Really?" Nic said, sounding interested. "When're you introducing me to her again?"

"She makes me stutter," Reed muttered, deciding to ignore his roommate's smart ass comment. "And I don't stutter. I've never stuttered. I don't like how she makes me stutter."

"So ask her out," Nic suggested.

"Are you kidding me? Did you not just hear what I said?"

"Yeah, you said you're horny. So ask her out. Bag her from your system a couple times, and problem solved. No more stuttering. No more cold sweats. Sounds simple enough to me, man."

"Well, I can't."

"Why not?"

Because I don't want *to bag her from my system*, Reed didn't shout, though he really wanted to. He liked having Sophia in his system. He loved having her possess most of his thoughts. He didn't want some temporary resolution. He wanted happily ever after. But Nic, man of a million one-night-stands, would never understand that.

"Because," he muttered aloud. "I work with her. If she turns me down, I'll have to face that rejection every day. And she *would* turn me down. I'm telling you this woman is perfect." From a distance, she put off that classy, unapproachable air. But the closer he got to her, the more personable and touchable she became. And the more out-of-reach he placed her in his mind.

"You're not exactly chopped liver," Nic argued. "You read the *Wall Street Journal* every morning. You drink fancy imported coffee, which smells awful, by the way. And you've got that sick tofu crap sitting in our refrigerator. Plus, you wear a three-piece suit to work, and you're an accountant, for God's sake. That sure sounds like an OCD perfectionist to me."

As Reed sighed, Nic continued. "If the working together thing really bugs you, then come do advertising with me until you get her out of your system. Better yet, we'll both quit our jobs and start up a new firm together. How many times have I said that would be a kick-ass idea?"

Reed closed his eyes briefly. "Haven't you ever wanted something so bad, something you think you can't live without, but you're afraid to reach for it because you don't want to learn you'll never be able to grasp it?"

"Sure," Nic said. Reed pictured him shrugging his answer off. "I wanted a bike when I was nine. So I badgered my parents to death until Dad gave in, and I got it for Christmas."

Reed realized his friend was clueless. Nic had never been so hungry he'd dug through restaurant dumpsters for food. He'd never had a little sister whose life depended on him. He'd never had a parent who didn't care whether he lived or died. He didn't know what real need was. He'd never lived true pain.

Reed envied Nic's happy childhood in the suburbs with two parents, an older brother, and a Saint Bernard.

"Do you want me to ask her on a date for you?" Nic teased.

Reed made a face. "Yeah, would you, please?"

"Sure thing, buddy. Just point her out to me."

Reed laughed. "Wouldn't that be a sight if you came in here and asked her out for me? I'd be the laughingstock of the entire department."

"Hey, I'd do it."

"I'm sure you would. But trust me, it'd take a miracle to get Sophia Eschell to go out with me."

"Miracles happen every day."

Not to Reed Walker. "Yeah, whatever. Listen, I've got to get back to work."

"So do I. Thanks for taking care of Toffee for me."

"See you." Reed hung up, shaking his head. He took his

pills, swallowing them with a cup of cooled, imported coffee. Then he closed his eyes and thought of Sophia.

"Impossible," he murmured.

Opening his lashes, he returned to reality and reached for the file she'd set on his desk just as Myrna patched yet one more call through to him.

"Can't a guy get a break?" Muttering under his breath, he picked up. "Walker here."

He opened the file and started scanning numbers.

"Thaddeus Walker?"

His rarely-used first name coming through the speaker caught him off guard. "Yes. Who is this?"

"This is Sergeant Morrison with the Kansas City Police department."

Reed paused. Since he'd just spoken to Nic and knew he was fine, his first thought went to his sister. "Yes?" he said slowly, already trying to calm himself. He wasn't the type to panic, but a cold finger of dread suddenly clutched the back of his neck and managed to dig its claws into his windpipe.

"Your sister, Danielle, requested we call you for her."

"No." The file slipped from his hand and spilled off the desk, onto the floor. He surged to his feet. "What happened? Is she okay?"

"She's pretty shaken up. Got some bruises, a broken wrist, and maybe some cracked ribs. They're taking X-rays now."

"Where is she? What happened? Was she in a car accident?"

"We're over at St. Luke's. But listen—"

"I'll be right there."

He hung up and was out of his seat before the phone settled in its cradle. He grabbed his jacket off the back of his chair and charged for the door.

"Reed!?"

In the main workroom, he paused long enough to glance at his wide-eyed secretary. She'd come half out of her cubicle and looked like she was going to chase after him.

"I have to go," he rasped.

"But your four o'clock—"

"Cancel it." He looked around blindly, searching for the fastest escape. Then he patted his pockets. "Wallet."

After racing back into his office, he grabbed his billfold from his top desk drawer. Myrna had moved into the walkway when he exited, her eyes almost bulging from the sides of her glasses.

"Clean that in there, will you? Thanks." Without a backward glance, he sped down the hall.

"But what do I tell your four o'clock?" she called after him.

"Family emergency," he yelled over his shoulder.

He didn't care if he made a spectacle of himself, dashing down the hall like a madman. All he could think of was his sister, who he'd raised from a baby and shielded from an uncaring mother. She was his only family, his only true responsibility.

CHAPTER 2

Reed thought he'd never make it to the hospital. With rush hour beginning, he cussed through most of the trip, nearly rear-ending a flower delivery van in the process.

He parked at the emergency room exit and hurried inside. At the front counter, he asked for Danielle Walker. The two receptionists working must've remembered her, because they exchanged knowing glances. Then one turned to him.

"What's your name, please?"

"Reed Walker. Thaddeus Reed Walker. I'm her brother."

They glanced at each other again. "Yes. Sergeant Morrison said to expect you. Please follow me."

Reed's pulse lurched as he nodded his thanks. He trailed the woman, wishing she'd pick up the pace. "Do you know what happened? Is she okay?"

The nurse's step faltered and she sent him an anxious look over her shoulder. "I'll let Sergeant Morrison explain everything."

That would be a yes, she knew exactly what had happened and, holy shit, it was bad. What he really couldn't understand was why a police officer, not a doctor, needed to speak with him.

They passed a uniformed cop speaking quietly into his radio. He looked up as if he'd been waiting for Reed.

Glancing back at the officer, Reed demanded, "What's going on?"

The nurse stopped in front of an opened door and motioned him inside. He peered through the entrance, but all he saw was a curtain. He pushed it aside and finally found his sister. She sat upright on a cot, shaking and huddled under a tightly wrapped hospital blanket. Her knees were drawn up and nearly touching her chest with her arms clutched around them. Rocking herself, she gazed blankly ahead with a vacant, hollow expression.

Her face was powdery white, yet her eyes were rimmed with a brilliant red. A sling encased one arm. Reed could see the beginning of a blue cast wrapped around her thumb and knuckles.

"Danni!" He rushed to her and enveloped her into a large hug. "What happened? Are you okay?"

Her body tightened; he jerked back in surprise, immediately letting go. He'd forgotten the officer said she had cracked ribs.

But she didn't look up at him with pain, only a fear that stunned him. Then her lashes fluttered and her gaze filled with recognition. "Reed?" she whispered hoarsely.

"It's me, Dan." He frowned and wiped away the hair matted to her cheek. "What happened? Were you in a car accident?"

He knew he should've talked her into getting a safer car. He opened his mouth to berate himself when he noticed the marks on her neck. Ten perfectly-shaped fingerprint bruises dotted her throat like Morse code. He stepped back, looked up to her face, and forgot to breathe. She'd gone back to staring at the wall and rocking herself, completely unresponsive.

"Danni?" he whispered.

Someone came into the room behind him. He whirled to find the officer from the hallway. Glancing toward his sister, he swallowed, not liking the zombie trance she had going on. He returned his attention to the officer, an odd feeling swirling through his gut before it worked its way up his esophagus.

"Mr. Walker?"

"Yes."

The officer stuck out his hand. Reed shook with him and found an odd comfort in the other man's firm, dry grip.

"I'm Sergeant Morrison. I work in the sex crimes unit. I've been questioning your sister and..."

"Wait." Reed yanked his hand back. "The *what* unit?"

He glanced sharply at Danni. With his skin prickling and black spots forming in his vision, his breathing went wonky.

No.

No way.

This wasn't happening.

He turned back to the sergeant. "I'm sorry, which unit?"

Morrison licked his bottom lip and sent a brief wince toward Danni. "Mr. Walker, your sister was sexually assaulted today in her college dorm room."

Reed wrenched a step in reverse. "What?"

The officer glanced away, his eyes bleak with sympathy.

With one of the worst fears of his life confirmed, Reed took a second to deny. This couldn't happen. Not to him. Not to Danni. He'd raised his sister so cautiously. He'd always been there to see to her safely. For God's sake, he hadn't let her cross a street without holding his hand until she was twelve. She was his responsibility. And Reed Walker looked after and took care of his responsibilities.

The officer was wrong. Just...wrong. That's all there was to it. Someone had made a huge mistake. No one would hurt his Danni, his sweet, gentle, childlike Danni.

But after studying her pale face, he knew it had to be true.

He'd failed her.

Nausea rose in his throat. His eyes burned but remained dry. He thought he might be sick.

He turned to Morrison for help. "She..." He tore a hand through his hair. "When? Where? *Who* did this?" He didn't bother to wait for an answer but grabbed his sister by the shoulders. "Danni, what happened?"

She gasped and looked up at him. Then she realized who he was as if she hadn't known he was there before. "Reed?"

"Danni?" He patted her hair helplessly, vividly remembering when she was a little girl and had always run to him for help. She looked up at him now with eyes begging for deliverance.

Why hadn't he been there for her?

"Danni," he said again. His voice cracked. "How could this happen to us?"

"I'm sorry," she said.

"No. Don't." He shook his head, tried to keep from bursting into tears. But his face felt hot.

Pulling her to his chest, he wrapped his arms tightly around her. She sobbed, and he quietly swayed with her, holding her and letting her tears collect on his suit jacket.

"I'm sorry," she mumbled again.

"Shh, no. I'm the one who's sorry, Danni. Shh."

Trembling, she put her undamaged arm around him, her fingers bunching a handful of his jacket's polyester cotton blend. Reed closed his eyes and rested his cheek on top of her hair. She felt so small. She was too fragile for this. He should've been able to prevent it.

Morrison stood awkwardly in the doorway, watching them. When Danni had spent out most of her tears for the time being, she said into Reed's chest, "I'm tired."

He glanced at the sergeant for permission. The officer shrugged and then nodded.

"All right," Reed said. "We're going to lay you down here on this cot for a few minutes, and then you're coming home with me, okay?"

"Okay." She let him help her down onto the mattress. As he tucked the blanket in around her, she closed her eyes.

Reed ran a hand over her cheek. Her skin was soft, smooth. Imagining someone viciously attacking her had him setting his jaw. When he turned to Morrison, his eyes were like granite and his mouth a firm slash of fury.

"I want answers." He motioned them out into the hall.

Morrison briefed him on what had happened, skimming over the details. By the time he was done, Reed leaned his forehead against the brick wall and tried to breathe normally. Danni had been in the shower. The rapist had knocked on the door, and she'd answered it in her bathrobe. He'd pushed his way inside and attacked.

The only good part of the story was that a girl in the dorm next door had heard the commotion and called the campus police. Danni's rapist was now behind bars.

"Mr. Walker?"

Reed rolled around and braced his back against the concrete wall to eye Morrison with numb blankness.

"I've already questioned her, and the doctors have collected a rape kit. Your sister is free to go for now. But, once the trial comes up, we'll need her to testify."

Reed nodded. "Okay."

"Do you think she'll be able to take the stand against him?"

With a vague nod, he murmured, "She'll do it."

Morrison gave him a small, disbelieving smile. "Are you sure? Some women can't even bring themselves to be in the same room as—"

"Danni can do it," Reed interrupted sharply.

He didn't want to think about this just now. He wanted to go to his sister.

Rubbing his eyes, he sighed and took a deep breath. "I'm sorry; I don't mean to be rude. This is hard to take in."

Morrison nodded. "It's all right. No apology necessary. Here's my information." He handed Reed a business card. "I've written down the case number on the back. If you have anything else that may be useful, please call. I think I've asked her everything for now. But another officer will be in touch with a subpoena to let her know when she needs to appear in court for her testimony."

"Okay." Reed stared at the card. "I'm taking her home with me."

"That's probably best. No one's allowed in her dorm room

until all the evidence is collected anyway. So if you need clothes or anything for her, call first. If we're not finished, we'll have an officer go in with you."

Reed nodded. He stuck the card in his jacket's inner pocket. "Okay. Thanks." He noticed his collar was still damp from Danni's tears.

Closing his eyes, he clenched his teeth and tried to control the rush of emotion. He balled his hands into fists. Though he was far from okay, he felt recovered enough to at least mask his thoughts.

Morrison watched him intently. "The doctors have already left some pamphlets with her, places she can call for help and counseling. I strongly recommend you urge her to contact them. After an event like this, the shock is almost overbearing. She'll need help."

Reed nodded because he couldn't seem to speak. He thanked Morrison again and turned to reenter Danni's room. She lay in exactly the same position as when he'd left her, eyes closed and body stiffly curled in the fetal position.

A fresh wave of sorrow gripped him as the sterile smell of hospital disinfectants grew suffocating.

He fell into the chair next to the bed and wiped the back of his palm over his mouth with shaking hands. His sister looked frail, beaten. It caused a bloom of anger and anguish to rip into him so sharply his body vibrated with repressed tension.

He wanted to hit something. He wanted to face the monster who had hurt her and rip his worthless head off. Reed's fingers curled until blunt nails dug into his palms.

This was wrong. It was all wrong. Danni couldn't suffer through such a tragedy twice in her life, though fortunately she probably didn't even remember the first experience.

He wished he'd been struck with the same amnesia.

Nausea welled in his stomach, and Reed doubled over, jamming his face between his knees until he could breathe. Memories flooded him. Even as he fought them back, they overtook his thoughts and plagued him with a horror he only visited in his darkest nightmares.

CHAPTER 3

Reed's roommate whistled as he breezed through the front door of their sprawling apartment. They'd bought the fixer-upper together fresh out of college, then had remodeled, redesigned and tinkered on every room until the place had become both their homes. And despite the fact that they now made enough money to live on their own, neither man felt inclined to move out.

Briefly shutting his eyes as Nic came inside, Reed swallowed, wishing for the first time that he lived alone so he could have a little more privacy to collect his scattered thoughts.

Nic paused, lifting his eyebrows. "Now, there's a rare sight. The ultimate workaholic, Reed Walker, is actually sitting on the couch, watching the boob tube. How's it feel, buddy? Your ass growing accustomed to those nice, soft cushions yet?"

Reed looked up, dazed. "What?"

His roommate nudged a finger toward the television where a man on the screen tried to sell some handy-dandy food vacuum. Then he laughed. "Overcome by the urge to shop?"

Reed glanced slowly to the flat screen. "Oh." He raised the remote and flipped the station to the news. Then he tossed the control onto the coffee table and swept both hands over his tired face.

Nic turned away, slipping a bottle of wine from the paper bag he'd carried in. "Did Toffee call?" He inspected the label before opening the freezer and setting it in an empty ice tray.

"No," Reed mumbled from the couch. Then he changed his mind. "I mean, yeah. I think so, maybe. Someone left a message."

Nic frowned and glanced toward the answering machine where a red light flashed. He shifted his gaze to Reed and closed the freezer door. "Is...uh...everything okay?"

"No." Reed closed his eyes, trying to block the concern in his friend's gaze.

He heard Nic shift hesitantly toward him. "What's going on? Looks like you've been hit by a bus."

"Feels worse," Reed croaked. "What am I going to do, Nic?"

Nic edged his way into the living room and sat gingerly on the arm of a side chair. "Did something bad happen?"

Reed tried to swallow and found he couldn't. He nodded. "Yeah, something bad happened."

"What?"

Reed opened his mouth, but just as quickly shut it. He shook his head.

Nic snapped his fingers and grinned. "I've got it. You finally asked Sophia out." He laughed, but Reed didn't join in.

He leaned down with an ashen face and buried his head between his knees, telling himself not to hyperventilate.

"Walker?" Nic shook his shoulder. "What's going on?"

"My sister," was all Reed could rasp.

Nic reared back. "Danni?" No one knew how important Danni was to Reed like Nic did, but even he could never truly understand the intensity of their bond. "What happened? Is she okay? Was she in a car accident?"

Reed sat up and cracked off a harsh laugh. "A car accident?" He ran his hand through his hair, messing it up until he probably looked like a wild man, though from the unstable coil in his stomach, he felt plenty wild without the new do. "You know, that's exactly what I thought when they first called me. Now I wish she *had* been in a freaking car accident."

Nic made a face. "Huh?" Then he froze. "Wait. She's still... alive, isn't she?"

Reed nodded. "Yeah, but I don't think she wants to be."

Nic shook his head. "Excuse me?"

"She was attacked," Reed said savagely. "Someone forced his way into her dorm room at school and forced himself on...forced her to...He took my little sister and ripped her apart, okay?" His body shuddered as he expelled a shaky breath.

Nic fell back into the chair, sitting heavily. "No." It looked like the air had been knocked out of him. "When?"

"Today." Reed picked up the remote again and began flipping through stations. "I got the call right after I talked to you."

Nic blew out a cheek full of air. "Wow. Man, I'm sorry. Do they know..." He swallowed and tried again. "Do they know who did it?"

Reed nodded. "Yeah. Cops caught him in the act. He's in jail right now."

Nic's shoulders slumped. "Well, that's good news at least."

Reed's hand fisted on the remote control and the channels started to zip by. Yeah right, real good news. His sister was *so* lucky. "She was only wearing a bathrobe."

Nic winced.

"I can't take this," Reed shouted and threw the remote.

The handheld hit a wall and fell to the floor. Both men watched the back pop off and a pair of batteries roll out.

Nic sat tense and quiet for a moment, watching Reed go through the worst turmoil of his life. "I...I don't know what to say."

Reed was about to tell him there was nothing *to* say when the guest bathroom door eased opened.

Nic's eyes bulged when Danni stepped out. He surged to his feet and stumbled backward, almost sprawling over the side of the chair. As soon as he caught his balance, he straightened and stared stupidly.

At twenty-one, Danni was normally cute, petite, active, and happy. She was always happy. Seven years younger than Reed, she possessed the pure, blissful demeanor of a child.

Today, she looked old and worn and traumatized. Her wet hair was down. She never wore it down. The limp pitch-black ends brushed against the top of her shoulders, soaking wet spots on the huge shirt she huddled inside, an old shirt of Reed's he sometimes wore around the house. The baggy sweats were his too. They were purple with a white wildcat emblem on the thigh.

She looked ultra-small in his clothes, and ultra-delicate. Her face was colorless except for the two red raccoon rings around her eyes. Her throat was dotted with bruises. It looked like someone had stamped his fingerprints on her neck with red ink. She held her casted arm over her stomach as if trying to shield herself from the world.

When she spoke, hardly a sound came out. But Reed could tell by the way her mouth moved she said, "Dominic."

Nic stuffed his hands in his pockets and shifted from one foot to the other. "Hey, kid. How're you doing?" As soon as the words left his mouth, a sick expression filled his face.

Reed shook his head. *How're you doing?* That answer was just a little obvious.

Nic must realized his *faux pas* too because he looked toward Reed for help, and Reed noticed Danni did the same thing.

He sighed and rubbed at a spot on the center of his forehead. When he looked up, his gaze was for Nic. "Danni's going to stay here for a while."

"Oh..." His roommate looked back toward Danni. "Umm...sure, sure. Whatever you need."

It was almost spooky, the way she stood perfectly still. Reed couldn't even tell when she blinked. When she looked Nic's way, a slow glide of her lashes was all that told him she'd turned her attention to his roommate. Her eyes stared with a dull lifelessness as if peering right through Nic.

Silently, she shifted her glance back to Reed. She looked toward his room and then back to him, wordlessly asking for permission with her gaze. He nodded, and then slowly, like a creaking hinge, she turned. She hobbled into his room, limping on her right foot, and quietly closed the door behind her.

When it latched shut, Nic immediately rounded on Reed. "Why didn't you tell me she was here?" he demanded in a harsh whisper.

Reed looked up. "What?"

"You could've warned me she was here. So I could prepare."

"Prepare for *what*?"

Nic lifted his hands, looking clueless. "I don't know. Some warning would've been nice, that's all. When you hear about something like that happening to someone and then, bam, there they are, it kind of shocks you, you know. I had no idea what to say to her. Or how to act."

"You didn't have to say anything. I'm sorry I didn't tell you she was here. *Your feelings weren't exactly a top priority to me.*" Disappointed and irritated by Nic's reaction, Reed shook his head. "Look, if you don't want her here, I'll get us a hotel room somewhere."

"No," Nic was quick to say. He sighed and ran his hand through his hair. "I didn't mean that. I just...I was shocked, okay? She can stay as long as she needs to. I'm sorry for overreacting." He glanced around the room, no doubt searching for an escape outlet. He saw the phone and focused on the blinking message light.

"Look. Why don't I get out of your hair tonight? You don't need me hanging around, making things uncomfortable."

Or rather, he didn't want to stick around, *feeling* uncomfortable, Reed thought sourly. But he nodded his understanding.

"I know it's no consolation at all, but I'm really sorry, Walker. If you need anything, just...Well, I'll be here for you."

Reed looked away. "Thanks," he said in a broken voice.

Nic hurried to the phone and listened to his message. Afterward, he scooped his briefcase off the counter and slipped into his bedroom. When he exited, he'd changed into jeans and a shirt and carried his sneakers in one hand. He bade Reed a goodbye and grabbed his keys on his way through the kitchen.

As soon as he closed the door behind him, Reed turned back to the television and stared blankly at the screen, empty and abandoned.

CHAPTER 4

Already garbed in her lounging clothes—boxers and an old worn black tank top—Sophia jumped when her phone rang. Not wanting to leave her nestled spot on her futon in front of the television, she twisted her torso and stretched behind her to reach her Droid sitting on the end table.

The tub of Ben and Jerry's in her lap tilted, and she had to catch it with her free hand to keep the melted sides from dumping a stream of ice cream all over her knee and into the crack between her cushions.

"Hello," she said distracted, both hands full, keeping her mind occupied elsewhere and not on the conversation.

But a slurring male voice caught her attention when he cooed, "'Sup, baby girl?"

She frowned and straightened. "I'm sorry. I think you have the wrong number."

"No, wait. Sophie?"

She paused. "Yes. Who is this?"

"It's Si."

"Sigh?" She frowned. Then, "*Silas?*"

Wow, she hadn't heard from Silas Varner for almost two years, not since he'd left her because she'd asked him to go into rehab.

"Yeah, it's me. Whatcha doing?"

Her instant smile over hearing a voice from the past faltered. "What're *you* doing, Si?" If he was drunk again, she'd murder him. "You sound—" *totally plastered.*

"Oh, right. Sorry about that. I don't think I've slept for thirty-six hours now. I just made it into town on a flight from Paris. I'm living in California, and since I was passing through, I thought I'd stop in and see you if you were around. Do a little catch up."

Let's see. It was after nine on a Friday night. Of course, Si would assume she'd be home.

Sophia blew out a breath. He'd always taken her for granted. She'd stayed with him for six months, during the worst of his alcoholism after his mom died. But when she'd asked him to seek help or leave, he'd left.

"I finished rehab about a month ago," he said, cutting into her thoughts, making her sit up with immediate interest.

"You...wait. You what?" He'd gone to rehab? For her? She popped to her feet and ran a hand through her rumpled hair.

On the other end of the line, Silas let out a chuckle. "Yep. I'm clean and sober. And I wanted to see you. I have a surprise."

The last time she'd seen him, Silas had asked her to marry him, and she'd said no, not unless he was willing to try rehab.

Her mind whirled.

A surprise?

She paced the length of her living room and back again.

All she could picture was him decked out in a tux and kneeling on one knee with a sparkling diamond in his hand as she opened her apartment door to receive him.

She swallowed. A surprise? Good Lord, was the man going to propose? Again?

"Uh..." A year ago, she would've said yes. Tonight, at nine on a Friday night, she could only remember how dry-witted he could be, how he left disgusting splatters on her toilet seat, and how much he'd always wanted her to do things with him she

she'd had no interest in. Baseball games were just not her thing.

But if he'd gone to rehab for her...

Her heart thumped hard against her chest. Did Silas really think she was important enough to induce him to enter rehab in order to get her back?

"Soph?" he said. "You still there, baby girl?"

"Y-yes. Sorry." She let out a nervous laugh, wincing because she hated it when he called her baby girl. "I'm here. I mean...I'm home if you want to stop by. It'd be great to see you again."

"Great." She could hear the smile in his voice. "I'm at the airport, so...be there in an hour?"

"Sure. I'll be here."

As they hung up, she sprang into action. Silas was coming. Silas, who'd braved rehab for her, was coming to her house, possibly to propose—an idea which panicked her to death.

She glanced down at her lounging clothes.

"Oh, sweet mercy," she muttered, and sprinted down the hall to her bedroom.

She only had one hour to prepare. Skidding through the doorway, she groaned as she took in the sight of clothes and bedding strewn across her room.

First things first. She made the bed. Then she scooped up a heaping pile of clothes and tossed it into her closet, shutting the door and closing the disaster inside. After she dashed to a drawer, dug out a relaxed outfit—relaxed enough to make Si think she hadn't dressed specifically for him—but something that looked nice, she zipped toward the bathroom.

As she stepped under a hot spray in her shower, her heart thumped hard against her chest.

Silas wasn't a dream come true. He certainly wasn't Reed Walker in the looks department, and he didn't have the best personality she'd ever met. But, wow oh wow, no one had ever made such a sacrifice for her.

She couldn't help but wonder, if he did proposed tonight, how in the world was she going to answer?

~ * ~

It was almost ten o'clock when Reed checked on Danni. He'd waited as long as he could, hoping she'd sleep for a while. She needed the rest. But when he opened the door and light from the living room spilled across his bed, he found her sitting on top of the sheets, her bruised eyes open and dazed.

Though he wasn't hungry himself, he was sure both of them had gone too long without sustenance. So he'd choked down an overripe banana that Nic had left sitting around and made her a small meal.

He carried in a tray full of hot tomato soup, a grilled cheese sandwich, and a cold cup of milk. When she was younger, nothing could cheer Danni like grilled cheese and soup.

Reed didn't know what he thought to accomplish by fixing her the meal now. But he did, anyway, in the vain hope of seeing her smile with the memory.

He pushed the light switch on with his shoulder. But when Danni winced at the harsh illumination and blinked repeatedly, he shrugged it back off. Using the tray to nudge a few magazines, reading glasses, and a tissue box aside on his nightstand so he could set the food down, he flipped on his nightlight, relieved when the shade muting the brightness didn't appear to hurt her eyes.

Then he sat beside her and studied her face. "I brought you some food."

She glanced over and studied the meal with the same bland expression he'd seen since he'd picked her up from the hospital. "Thank you."

Reed brushed some stray tendrils out of her face. The black locks had dried into a twisted mess. "You forgot to comb your hair." He worked out a few knots with his fingers.

"I didn't have my brush."

He nodded. "I didn't think of that. I'll pick up a few of your things tomorrow."

She didn't respond. His hand dropped from her hair. He

watched her for a moment, and his heart cracked open. He couldn't take much more of this. He just wanted her to look at him and smile like his Danni did. He wanted her to laugh or scream, or cry, or *something*. Anything had to be better than this blank, unending nothingness.

A tightness worked its way into his chest, and he knew he had to leave before he started to bawl.

"Well." He smoothed down a wrinkle on her sleeve. "At least try to eat something. I'll be back in a while to check on you."

He stood.

"Reed?"

Pausing, he glanced over. She'd turned her head toward him, so he sat back down. "Yeah?"

"You told Dominic."

He frowned. His mouth worked. "I…I what?"

"You told Dominic what happ—" She paused as if she was choking before she regained her whispering voice. "—what happened to me."

A painful knot formed in Reed's chest. He'd been trying to please her all evening. He'd been so careful to make her comfortable, to provide her with anything she needed, to make her smile. But instead, he'd upset her.

"He's my roommate," he blurted out. He told Nic almost everything. "He needed to know why you were here."

"I don't want anyone to know."

"But, Danni—"

"Please don't tell anyone else." She reached blindly for him.

He caught her hand and held on. "Danni, no one is going to think badly of you. You don't have to be ashamed."

Her fingers clamped around his, and she started to shake. A tear trickled down her check. "But it's so…it's so much. Too much. I don't want anyone else to know. Please, Reed." More tears fell.

He panicked. "Okay, Dan. Okay. I won't tell anyone else."

"No one at all."

"No one at all. I swear it."

She nodded and sniffed. Her fingers remained clamped around his. "And Dominic?"

"I'll make sure he keeps quiet. We won't tell anyone if you don't want us to."

"I don't." She hiccupped and shuddered. "I don't want anyone to know."

Reed nodded, but he couldn't speak. He finally managed a shaky, "Okay. It's fine. No one will know."

"Thank you. You're the only person who could understand." Her fingers loosened and she turned away, back into a place inside herself, far from him and the world.

He stared at her a moment, wondering what she meant by that statement. What did she remember?

Panic rose inside him until he couldn't control himself any longer. He rushed for the door and out into the living room, but that wasn't release enough either. He strode to the window of the apartment, yanked it open and climbed out onto the rickety metal fire escape.

The cool night air washed over him. He gritted his distress into the street and grabbed the railing of the escape, shaking it, trying to rattle loose the rage, and the pain, and the fear. The platform swayed under him until he hung his head. It was then that he wondered why he'd ever quit smoking.

CHAPTER 5

Eleven o'clock came and passed before Sophia's doorbell chimed.

She'd straightened up the living room and stashed her melted ice cream back in the freezer. Then she'd nestled herself on the couch and practiced looking relaxed, when in truth, her heart beat against her ribcage like a mini drummer for some crazy heavy metal band had taken up residence inside her chest.

When Si's I'll-be-there-in-an-hour promise didn't pan out, her nerves wrung themselves out even more. He was late—typical Si—and most likely drunk somewhere.

Two hours later, she was dead asleep, slumped against her couch cushions with her head tilted wonkily to the side. The bell pealed two, possibly three times before she even stirred. On the fourth ring, she sprang into a sitting position with a gasp.

He was here.

Using her socks to slide halfway across the hardwood floor and into the hallway, she came to a stop in front of her door. Then, wondering why she was wearing socks to greet an intimate visitor, she yanked both stockings off her feet and stuffed them in the umbrella holder urn sitting by the exit. Fortunately, her toenails had recently been painted, and the crimson polish made her toes look sexily adorable.

After smoothing back her hair, brushing down her clothes and wiping her fingers over her face, desperately hoping she didn't have sleep lines on her cheek, she reached for the doorknob.

A single twist later, she pulled open the door, and there he stood.

Wow, the past two years had been good to him. He actually looked like he'd just come from Paris, all sleek and sophisticated with pressed slacks and a collared polo. Even his hair looked styled and gelled. The Silas Varner she had known never put gel in his hair.

His grin was familiar though, genuine and wide. "Hey, baby girl." He opened his arms and stepped into her apartment, enfolding her into a hearty, crushing hug.

Sophia closed her eyes and sank against him, relishing the texture of human contact. How long had it been since she'd experienced a simple hug?

He smelled different. Classier. Kind of like she imagined Paris might smell.

Excitement stirred in her belly. Maybe Si really had changed, maybe he was better. Maybe she could actually marry a man who'd gone through so much change and growth for little ol' her.

"Sorry, we're late. We both wanted to stop by the hotel and clean up a little after the flight before coming over."

Sophia froze, then pulled back. "We?"

"*Oui*," he answered, his pun making his grin turn ornery. Eyes dancing with pride and excitement, Si stepped out of the doorway to let the woman standing behind him into the apartment. "Soph," he introduced. "This is my surprise. I want you to meet Gabriella. My wife."

Sophia pressed her lips tightly together, hoping her face was completely blank of emotion. "Wife," she echoed, before forcing a wide smile and sticking out her hand. "Hello."

Grasping Gabriella's slim, limp palm and trying to ignore the huge rock sticking up from her ring finger, she dropped her jaw and turned to Si. "Oh, my God. I can't believe you're married."

Masking her shock with, well, *shock*, she gave Silas another hug, letting him think it was happy, congratulatory shock instead of the other kind.

"Thanks." He glowed as he pulled away and snagged his wife's hand.

Gabriella looked French, like a French model in fact. Her blond hair was smoothed to the side away from her forehead. Her eyes were large and soulful and her mouth was small and puckered. The woman looked like she could do with a little more meat on her bones. Sophia would've been glad to share some of hers.

"I wanted Gabby to meet you," Silas was saying, "since you're the one to give me that initial push to straighten my life out."

Sophia turned to him, thinking that wasn't quite how she recalled it. She remembered the push, sure, but the straightening-out-his-life part had not followed. Not until after he'd left her, obviously.

Bitterness burned through her gut, but she continued to smile as Gabriella clasped her arm. With a charming French accent, she spoke. "After Silas talked about his dear friend, Sophia, so ardently and how she helped him through his decline, I felt I must meet you in person and thank you for making him the man he is today."

His dear friend Sophia?

Silas had called her his dear friend?

Friends with benefits maybe, Sophia wanted to mutter, when honestly they'd been so much more. Friends didn't practically move in together. Friends didn't propose marriage.

Where did Si get off calling her a *friend*?

Gabriella leaned confidentially closer. "For a while, I feared you might have had a love affair with him. But now that I meet you, I know that cannot be."

Insulted beyond measure, Sophia gasped. Stunned speechless, she turned to gape at Silas. He flushed and coughed into his fist. Then sweeping his arm over his wife's shoulder, he finally met her gaze. "Well, it was great to see you again. I didn't want to pass through town without saying hi."

Somehow remembering her manners, Sophia got a grip and shook herself back into her role as hostess. "Uh…" Ushering the newlyweds toward her front room, she said, "Come on in. Can I get you two anything to drink?"

Husband and wife frowned. Gabriella narrowed her eyes and lifted her nose, haughtily announcing, "Silas no longer drinks."

Sophia blinked. Then flushed. "I…I didn't mean alcohol. I just…*tea*! Would either of you like a nice cold glass of sweet tea?"

Silas saved her from her fumbling and smiled graciously. "Actually, we need to be going. Our flight out departs early in the morning. The only reason we're actually staying overnight is because Gabs doesn't like to sit too long on a plane. The trip from Europe to the states was almost more than she could take."

Sophia could've been as nasty as she felt and smarted something demeaning back, but instead she frowned as if sorry to see them go. "Are you sure you can't come in and talk for a while?"

Si nodded and pulled her into one last hug. "You take care, baby girl," he said into her ear. "Keep in touch, will you?"

She smiled. "Of course." *Not on your life, pal.*

And then they were gone.

Sophia stared at the closed doorway for a good minute before she sputtered, "Did that really just happen? Seriously?"

She wasn't sure what Si had been trying to prove. That he could survive without her? That he could clean himself up and find another woman even better than her?

"Look here, Sophia?" she spoke aloud for the absent Si as she slumped back into the living room. "I don't need you anymore. My Twiggy lookalike and I can live happily ever after without you. God." She groaned and slumped face first onto the futon cushions. "I'm such an idiot."

Sitting up, she ran both hands through her hair. "Never again," she said with renewed determination. "Never, never, *never* will I ever consider dating a man with any kind of baggage. I am *so* through with men."

~ * ~

Reed checked on his sister once more at midnight. Still awake, she hadn't moved but to roll onto her side where she now stared at a different wall. She hadn't touched her food. The soup sat crusted over and the sandwich lay cold and soggy. He sank onto the mattress beside her and touched her back.

"Danni, you need to eat."

"Okay," she rasped in a hoarse voice, but made no move toward the food.

He sighed. "Sit up."

She did, slowly.

Reed propped the pillows against the headboard so she could rest upright. He took one half of the sandwich, tore off a bite-sized piece, and brought it to her mouth. She opened, so he fed her.

Danni chewed like a cow, slow and monotonous, keeping it all in her mouth until Reed finally said, "Swallow."

She did.

He patiently went through the whole routine, feeding her each bite and reminding her to swallow until he was satisfied she'd had enough. She said nothing, never even looked at him. When she finished eating, he took the tray into the kitchen and cleaned the dishes.

He gave himself plenty of time, washing and drying, before he went back to her. He needed to get a hold of himself. He couldn't look at her without feeling furious and vulnerable. He couldn't sit by without wanting to break something. But he couldn't just leave her alone either.

When he returned, she was the same. He pulled the

blankets out from under her and then settled them on top of her prone body. All the while, he ordered in a gentle tone. "Lie down...Now close your eyes."

She followed every command.

He went to his dresser and hunted up a comb. When he ran it through her hair, she didn't make a sound, didn't even give him a signal that she felt a thing or if he hit a knot; she merely stared mutely at the far wall.

"Remember your first day of school?" he asked. "You wanted to have your hair braided into two tails. I didn't know anything about braiding, so I pulled it into one pony tail." He gave a quiet chuckle and looked down at his hands. When had they started to shake? "We never did learn how to make a braid, did we?"

"No," she whispered.

He set the comb on the nightstand and stood, rubbing his fingers over his eyes. Taking a seat in a chair in the corner, he fisted his hand and brought his knuckles to his mouth. "Sleep now, Danni. I'll watch over you."

After a while, she did. But it wasn't easy or restful. Her body would occasionally jerk or her breathing would turn choppy. Sometimes, she'd gasp awake, clawing at her throat. Reed stuck around, his stomach knotting with tension. He always rushed to her when she woke. Then he talked to her in a soothing, quiet voice until she drifted again.

Once, she sat straight up in bed and said something garbled and unintelligible. But the tone of her voice was clear enough. It screamed fear, desperation, agony.

Reed had been nodding off, but stumbled to his feet. He tripped to her and asked if she wanted something to drink. She declined, but he got her a glass of water anyway. He held the cup while she drank. When she finished, he set the drink aside.

Mechanically, she lay back down and closed her eyes.

He studied her face, waiting for her eyes behind their thin, bruised lids to move back and forth. When he was sure she was out, he made his way through the dark, into the living room, where he collapsed onto the couch.

The click of the front door had Reed swiveling his head around to watch Nic slip inside. His roommate quietly eased his way through the living room until he noticed Reed sitting up and awake.

He paused. "Why're you sitting in the dark?" He clicked on a floor lamp. "You hate the dark."

Nic knew better than to call Reed's aversion *fear*. He'd testily corrected Nic the first time he'd seen Reed plug a nightlight into an outlet next to his dorm bed. They'd known each other all of five minutes and were unpacking their belongings to room together for their first semester of college.

Nic had grinned and asked, "What? You afraid of the dark?"

"I'm not afraid," Reed snapped back. "I just don't like it."

Yet, here he was, shrouded in dark. As the dim lamplight flared between the two men, Reed knew his friend could see the exhaustion lining his face. He felt so goddamn tired.

"How's it going?" Nic asked quietly.

Reed took another deep breath. "It hasn't been a good night."

His roommate winced sympathetically. "No, I don't guess it has."

Reed leaned his head against the back of the couch and closed his eyes. Nic nudged his leg with a toe.

"Why don't you get some sleep, bud? I got a feeling everything's going to be the same in the morning. So what'll it matter if you get a few Z's or not? Huh?"

"I'm not tired."

"Sleep anyway."

"What if she wakes?"

"If she needs you, she'll come and get you. Look. Walker. Tomorrow's not going to be fun either. Get some rest before you have to suffer through it."

Reed scrubbed as his face. "I need a cigarette."

Nic shook his head and stuck his hands in his pockets. "You're not going to start that again, are you?"

"I've never wanted one so bad in my life."

"Well, tough. You threw away your last pack five years

36

ago."

"Yeah." Reed sighed and exhaled as if he was blowing out a lungful of nicotine. The craving to escape into that smoke-filled haze was overwhelming. He'd do anything for just a little relief to calm all the disorder inside him.

"Sleep," Nic commanded quietly. "It's two in the morning. Time for some shut eye."

Reed couldn't help but notice Nic was treating him the same way he'd just treated Danni. He wondered if the man would be combing his hair and spoon-feeding him next.

God, he needed to get it together.

"Okay, I'll try." He yawned, proving he could manage some rest.

"Good. Sleep tight, man. Don't let the couch bugs bite."

"Douche," Reed muttered, suddenly wishing they'd turned one of their spare rooms into an actual guest room with an actual bed. He had a bad feeling he was going to grow an intimate knowledge of this sofa before the next few weeks were over.

Nic let out a low laugh and started toward his room. Before he disappeared inside, Reed remembered the promise he'd made. "Hey, Calhoun."

Nic paused, his hand on the doorknob. "Yeah?"

"You haven't told anyone, have you? About Danni."

His roommate frowned. "No. Why?"

"Don't. She doesn't want anyone to know. She flipped out about me telling you. So keep it quiet, will you?"

"Sure, I guess. No problem."

With his one mission for the evening complete, Reed lay down on the couch. But even as worn down as he was, hours passed before he began to drift. And even when he did, his own nightmares jerked him awake in a sweaty panic.

CHAPTER 6

Sophia gnawed on her bottom lip as she re-crossed her legs for about the tenth time in the past five minutes. Winding a lock of hair around her finger, she idly glanced at her coworkers. They seemed to be mesmerized with similar expressions of abject boredom.

The meeting they were scheduled to have was supposed to begin ten minutes ago—oops, make that eleven minutes ago. Their not-so-great and certainly not-mighty leader, Marcus, was supposed to be starting their happy gathering, but yeah, he merely sat at the table with the rest of them, arms crossed over his chest as he glared at the clock.

Finally, Sophia cleared her throat. "Marcus, do you want me to find out where he is?"

Everyone knew who *he* was. Though his name hadn't been mentioned, it was obvious to all that nothing happened on the accounting floor of Kendrick Advertising without the leadership of one Reed Walker.

"No," Marcus bit out stubbornly, his jaw set in a hard line. "I want *him* to remember and get his tail in here himself."

Sophia held in a dramatic sigh. Lord above. Could anyone

be more pathetic than Marcus Weatherby?

She seriously doubted it.

"Are you sure he's even here today?" she asked, trying to be diplomatic.

She wasn't quite able to mask the irritation in her voice though, and Marcus sent her a dirty look. "Where else would he be?"

Sophia rolled her eyes. Yes, she actually rolled her eyes at a superior. But after the weekend she'd had, the man was lucky she was being so pleasant. Besides, this was Marcus they were talking about. The only person she knew who could handle him with any sort of tact was Reed, and Reed was obviously AWOL.

"Just a guess," she said, "but maybe he took the day off."

Reed was human, after all. He surely needed at least one day off in his lifetime. Sophia was sure the man had plenty of sick and vacation leave to spare. She'd yet to see him use either.

"A day off?" Marcus repeated dumbly. He frowned at Sophia as if she'd lost her mind before he barked, "Don't be stupid. Walker knows the Brunetti case needs to be finished today. There's no way he'd be somewhere else."

Huffing out a breath, Sophia thought up a biting comment to smart back. But before she could, she noticed everyone in the room had turned their attention to her as if they expected a grand retaliation.

Irritated they knew her so well, she held her tongue and scowled back. It wasn't like she was worried about losing her job, though. Reed would never let Marcus fire her.

Okay, so he'd never come right out and told her, "*I would never let Marcus fire you*," but she knew instinctively he'd stick up for her. And whoever he stuck up for stayed employed.

She'd seen him defend other good employees before, and she knew she was on that list. She certainly wasn't as stupid as Marcus had just said.

Then again, it would be hard for Reed to back her today if he wasn't even present.

Attempting to pattern after the legendary-yet-absent Mr. Walker, she kept her thoughts to herself and gave Marcus a small smile, letting him win that round.

And so, the room once again fell into uncomfortable silence.

Five minutes later, she couldn't stand it any longer. Making an executive decision, she pushed to her feet. "I'm going to see if he's here. Maybe something came up."

Marcus opened his mouth to object, but Sophia ignored him and stalked to the door. Once she was in the hall, she slowed her pace, happy to be out of the meeting room and breathing fresh air again.

As she neared Reed's corner office, she slowed even more. His door was closed, a foreign sight all on its own. Then she noticed all the lights off inside.

Stopping at his secretary's desk, Sophia glanced around for Myrna. The older woman stood three cubicles over, chatting with another secretary. Okay, now she *knew* Reed had to be absent. There was no way Myrna would be away from her desk if he was around.

"Myrna," she called.

The woman paused her chitchatting to glance over.

"Is Reed in today?"

"No he's not, sugar. He left early Friday in a big hurry, saying something about a family emergency. I haven't seen him since."

Caught off guard by Myrna's answer, Sophia lifted her eyebrows.

Reed had family?

Well, of course he had family. He was human, after all. Humans tended to have families. But Sophia had always viewed him as a lone wolf who took care of himself and didn't need another soul on earth to survive. The mere mention of a family made him seem more mortal and a lot less of the outsider he put himself out there to be.

It made Sophia see him in a whole new light.

He was a family man. Huh. Who would've thunk it?

She faced his closed door and studied the nameplate reading *T. Reed Walker*. She wasn't sure why, but when he'd first started, she'd been determined to discover what the T stood for.

Staring at that T now reminded her he *was* Thaddeus, and someone had named him that, someone in the same family having an emergency.

Sophia frowned. She hoped everything was okay. It had to be a fairly large emergency if it'd caused him to be absent.

Grinning, she realized she could laugh in Marcus's face and sing, "Ha, ha, I was right. He's gone." Not that she would do that, but there was satisfaction in knowing she could.

"Myrna," she called. "Is his office open? I want to see if Reed left a file sitting on his desk. We need it for a meeting we're having."

"Sure, honey. Help yourself. Marcus has already been in there this morning, snooping around."

Sophia winced. Gee, no wonder Reed never called in sick. His secretary obviously let any and every one pilfer through his things when he was gone. Humph. And Marcus claimed *Sophia* was a bad secretary.

But thinking of Marcus, she scowled. If he'd already been by Reed's office today, he obviously knew Reed was gone. Geez, what kind of point was he trying to make, forcing everyone to sit in the meeting room and wait for an employee he knew wouldn't show?

Pushing open Reed's door, she paused in the entrance. The room held a certain void that caused her skin to prickle. Without Reed's presence, it felt extra empty. Sophia held her breath as if she was stepping into a holy shrine. Quickly shaking off the heebie-jeebies, she hurried to his desk.

She knew her stars were aligning when she spotted the Brunetti file on top of his desk, lying open as if it were the last thing he'd been viewing before he'd left for his family emergency.

Sophia picked up the three sheets she found on the floor, tucked them into the folder, and closed it so she could hurry from the room. Shutting the door behind her, she clutched the dossier to her chest and returned to the meeting, where no one had moved since her departure.

Marcus sat up as she came inside.

"He's definitely gone," she announced. "But I have the Brunetti information right here, so we can—"

"Take it back!" Marcus snapped.

Sophia paused, her mouth falling open. "Excuse me?"

"It's Walker's case. We can't go on without him."

"But we close this account today. Kendrick needs this information by three."

Marcus nodded moodily. "We're *supposed* to close today, but obviously we can't now that *someone* decided not to show. We'll have to call for a delay."

Sophia opened her mouth again. They most certainly did not have to call for a delay. Marcus was the final authority. He could approve any account with or without Reed's presence. But she snapped her mouth shut when she saw him slice her a challenging scowl.

"Yes, sir," she bit out.

Marcus rose to his feet and addressed the rest of the room. "It's settled then. We'll meet again as soon as Walker decides to grace us with his presence."

And that was that.

Sophia returned the file to Reed's desk and the accounting department did not meet its deadline for the Brunetti account.

But Sophia wasn't as concerned about the account as she was about the elusive Thaddeus Reed Walker.

Where was the mysterious accountant and just what had been so awful to make him miss the closing of an important account?

~ * ~

Reed slammed down the phone just as Nic walked into the apartment. Letting out a healthy curse, he fisted his hands and took a deep, drawing breath.

"That good, huh?" Nic slipped off his shades and set them on his briefcase.

"My so-called boss," Reed answered. He rolled his eyes as he sneered, "He misses me."

Nic arched his brow skeptically. "Isn't that a good thing?"

"No," Reed snapped. "It means nothing's getting done around there, and nothing's going to get done until I go back."

Nic stretched his arms over his head and let out a loud yawn, appearing comfortable and relaxed, though he peeked a skittish glance Danni's way. "I bet he just called to see how much time he has to be in charge before you return and bully your way back into his spot."

Reed sent his roommate a dark scowl, silently telling him to shove it. He thrust his hands through his hair and took a few steps forward before he spun around and started the other way. But his restless pacing only made him more agitated.

He whirled toward Nic. "Can you stay here a few minutes? I have to go out. I need to get...I need to go out. I'll be right back."

Nic's gaze flashed toward Danni where she sat in the center of the couch. The expression he sent Reed spelled pure panic, but he cleared his throat and croaked, "Um...sure."

"Thanks." Reed grabbed his wallet and rushed out the door.

Fifteen minutes later, he returned and his system had calmed enough that at least he didn't want to rip his own flesh off with his fingernails.

Nic was still loitering in the kitchen, nervously tapping his fingers on top of the bar as he guzzled from an aluminum can.

From the couch where she hadn't moved either, Danni stared at him as if sizing up his power and strength, his ability to harm. She studied his hand that held the can, taking in his wide palm and each muscled finger.

Nic's chest wasn't as wide and deep as Reed's but he wasn't a shrimp by any stretch of the imagination. He was rangy and slim-hipped and could take her down easily. Hurt her. Reed knew his friend would never touch a hair on Danni's head. He knew she knew it too, but her eyes continued to warily follow every move Nic made.

Nic lowered the can and sighed. When he caught her watching him, he took a step back as if he was more frightened of her than she was of him.

An elephant yelping at the sight of a mouse.

"Thirsty?" he asked.

She shook her head.

Reed shut the door at his back loud enough to make both his sister and friend jump. They whirled their attention his way as if they hadn't realized he'd already returned.

Nic forced a tense grin. "Back already?" he said, though his eyes screamed, *what took you so freaking long?*

Nodding, Reed moved to the chair by the couch. He watched the television as if he hadn't left. But he suspected Danni could smell the cigarette smoke on him or see the outline in his pocket of the pack he'd just bought. She kept sending him worried glances. She had to know he was getting antsy because that night when he tucked her in like he had the past four nights, she told him he should go to work the next day.

He shook his head. "No, it's okay. Don't worry about them. They'll be fine without me."

"I'm not worried about them," she said. "I'm worried about you. Go to work tomorrow, Reed. Please. For me?"

~ * ~

Reed wasn't sure if he was ready for this or not but he showed up at Kendrick the next morning, ten minutes late. Everyone who knew who he was gawked as he strode by. He never called in sick. He never showed up late. And he never went without a tie. Not that he noticed his appearance or the time.

Marcus must've gotten wind of his arrival because he burst into Reed's office shortly after Reed entered it. Reed had barely sunk into his chair, and he hadn't even started to think about looking at his workload yet.

"Where have you been?"

Reed sighed. "I told you three times over the phone. I had a family situation."

"Well, it's about time you decided to show. There's an emergency meeting in ten minutes to make up for the one we missed Monday I had to cancel because of you. So you better be there."

Reed spread his arms wide, "I'm here, aren't I? Why would I miss it now?" He didn't need this today. He had a headache. He craved a cigarette.

Marcus glared. "Ten minutes. In the conference room. Don't forget."

Reed rolled his eyes. "I won't."

An expression of rage marred Marcus's face, but he didn't care.

Marcus didn't like him because he knew Reed should have his job. But that had never stopped him from always pushing off all his work onto Reed's lap. Therefore, Reed didn't understand what he had to be so upset about. If Marcus wanted to gain his own respect in the department, he'd get out of his office to do something besides complain for once in his life.

Reed showed up to the conference eleven minutes later and could almost see the steam rolling off Marcus's collar. He was the last to arrive and slid into the only empty seat available, which happened to be directly across from Sophia Eschell.

Seeing her was like spotting a hopeful rainbow after a nasty thunderstorm. Something inside him snapped. Intense and gripping, the feeling made Reed want to leap across the table, bury his face in her stomach and wrap his arms around her waist so he could bawl his eyes out.

She watched him, as did everyone else in the room, with frank curiosity. They all had to be wondering what had happened to him. Prompt, dependable Reed Walker was late to a meeting. What was the number for Guinness?

His attention landed briefly on Sophia. Her eyes, the color of finely aged whiskey, gave him a deep yearning to taste her skin just to see if it matched the flavor of her gaze. He looked away and dropped into his chair, hoping he hadn't stared too long.

Marcus cleared his throat.

Reed glanced up to catch the glare from his superior. He glared right back, crossing his arms over his chest.

"Now that everyone's here. *Finally*. We've got both the Brunetti and the Travis account to discuss." He went over a few brief things everyone in the room already knew.

Reed tuned him out and found himself looking at Sophia again. As she hastily jotted notes, he studied the top of her bent head. He loved her thick, light red hair.

His gaze roved on, sliding over her shoulders and down her arm. Her hand moved quickly as she scrawled. Her nails were long and painted a muted pink. They'd feel like heaven on him. He wanted those nails grazing his chest, his thighs, everywhere. He'd return the favor with his mouth and kiss her—

A vision of Danni entered his head. Reed winced, instantly guilty for such a horny daydream. His injured sister was at home alone, and his mind was in the gutter, thinking only of himself.

He wondered how she was getting along.

Maybe he shouldn't have left her by herself yet. She'd looked so scared and lost when he'd walked out the door this morning. He shifted in his seat, wondering if he should call—

"*Walker!*" Marcus boomed, dragging Reed's attention back to the meeting. His boss looked befuddled as he demanded, "What the hell is wrong with you?"

It'd take a week to explain everything wrong with him, so Reed merely scrubbed at his jaw, surprised it was rough and bristly. Hadn't he shaved this morning?

Clearing his throat, he murmured, "Come again?"

Marcus turned a bright, angry red. "You were the last one with that file. Are you finished with it yet?"

Reed squinted in confusion. "What file?"

"The file for the account we've been talking about for the last five minutes. I know I sent it your way." He glanced accusingly at Sophia.

Her eyes turned to Reed, wide and panicked. "I dropped it by your office," she said, her expression begging him to remember. "Last *Friday*."

He closed his lashes. "Oh." When he opened up and faced his supervisor, he was calm. "I haven't had a chance to look at it yet."

"My God, Walker." Marcus pounded on the table with his fist. Everyone except Reed pulled back and darted glances around the room as if looking for the best place to hide. "It was given to you to look through by Monday."

Reed stayed calm yet rigid. "Something came up," he said, amazed he sounded so casual with his teeth clenched hard enough to break every tooth in his mouth.

"Oh, right, I forgot," Marcus scoffed. "You had a *family* emergency."

He lost a little of his coolness as his eyes narrowed. "That's correct, I did."

"Well, why you were off playing with your family, we had a true emergency here, a deadline that didn't get met because *you* neglected to even look at that file."

"As I recall, I'm not the only person with the authority to close an account," Reed shot back. "It could've—and should've—been taken care of without me."

"It was on your desk. So it was your job."

"And it was on your desk before it was on mine," Reed returned. "You're the one who passed the buck, pal."

His boss went utterly still, his face freezing its expression. "What's that supposed to mean?"

"It means, Marcus, if you ever got off your fat ass and actually participated in our company with us, maybe you could look around and realize who's taking on most of the weight. It wasn't my job to review and sign off on the fucking account in the first place. I had to be gone for a few days, and you shouldn't have one word to say to about what I haven't done because, ultimately, it wasn't my responsibility."

A vein in Marcus's neck bulged and pulsed. People slid low in their seat as if they feared it would rupture and splatter them all. Not that Reed particularly cared. He swore steam had to be hissing from his own ears.

Marcus pointed a meaty finger. "You'll have that file reviewed by noon."

"And if I don't?" Suddenly he didn't care if he lost his job. Finishing the Brunetti account hadn't been his responsibility. *Danni* had been his responsibility, and he'd been too involved here to be there for her.

"I can review it," Sophia piped up.

Reed's head twisted around so fast she jumped back and gasped as he pinned her with a lethal stare.

"*I'll* review it," he snapped, though he instantly felt awful for taking his anger out on her. His voice softened. "The point I was trying to make is that it wasn't my job. And it's not yours." He nodded his head toward Marcus. "It's *his*. And he had no right to pounce on me because, for once in my life, I didn't do his work for him."

He pushed his chair back and stood.

"Where do you think you're going?" Marcus demanded.

"I have a file to read," Reed muttered and strode toward the exit, letting the door bang shut behind him.

CHAPTER 7

When the meeting let out seconds after Reed departed, Sophia fled the conference room with the rest of the stunned employees. She glanced up and down the halls.

Already, the details of the argument were spreading. But she wasn't interested in dishing out rumors. She scanned the halls for the source.

Sophia had a natural tendency to care for the wounded. When she was little, she'd sneak stray, half-dead kittens into her bedroom and tend to them until they were fat and happy, or until her mother found them and off they went, mended or not.

Well, today her frail feline was named Reed Walker.

In all the time she'd known him, he'd never, *never* behaved like this before. Reed was one of the most even-tempered people she'd ever met. He didn't lose his cool. He never cursed or raised his voice. He never told anyone what he really thought. He kept himself polite, formal, and unreadable.

Something had to be terribly wrong, and it couldn't be mere annoyance with Marcus. Marcus was always annoying. Reed knew how to deal with him diplomatically. Something else had set him off. Something she was determined to discover. She had detected a raw pain in his eyes. When he'd first come into the meeting and looked at her, she saw it. The anguish in his gaze begged for relief. And Sophia couldn't ignore a plea like that. She decided no human that miserable should suffer alone.

She glanced both ways to see if anyone was watching her. They all seemed busy gossiping, so she eased up to Reed's office. As soon as she reached the doorway and glanced inside, she saw he wasn't around. After smiling at Myrna, who stopped her and asked what had happened, Sophia relayed a sketchy outline of the events and then quickly moved on.

Where could he be? He hadn't quit, had he? She tried the copier room, and even passed Marcus's office. The break room was the last place she expected him to be, but she knew he was there before she even reached the doorway. Two men ahead of her started to enter the lounge, only to stop dead in the entrance and then scurry off. "...*heard he actually punched Marcus in the jaw*..." Their words reached her as they passed.

Sophia had never known Reed to take a break or even grace the break room with his presence. When he had lunch, he either ate in his office or went out. So there was yet another reason she could tell something was way off kilter.

Halting in the doorway, she stole a moment to collect herself before entering. She didn't want to get her head bitten off for trying to help the wounded animal, but she hadn't gotten this far in the world by backing down from a possible confrontation either.

Courage bolstered, she strolled inside as if she didn't have a care in the world. He sat at a table, studying an open folder. It had to be the Brunetti file. After what he'd said in the meeting, he was still going to do Marcus's job. Her insides melted at his significant gesture. This was definitely a man of worth.

He picked up a smoking cigarette from the ashtray in front of him and brought it to his lips. The break room was the only place in the building where smoking was allowed. That explained what he was doing in here.

Still, her finely trimmed eyebrows arched.

"I didn't know you smoked."

His head popped up, and he nearly dropped the cigarette into his lap. He fumbled to steady his grip before his gray eyes moved up to her face. As she stepped into the break room, Sophia had to smile at the male appreciation in his gaze. She was used to men looking at her, but there was something entirely different about the way Reed Walker watched her. His brooding lids seemed so lonely as his gaze traveled down her figure.

He slid that same look away toward the cigarette in his hand. "I don't," he said, then corrected himself. "I mean, I quit." He glanced back to her as she sat across from him. "For a while, anyway."

She rested her hands on the table and folded them together, businesslike.

He settled back in his chair and let out a breath. "I'm sorry for snapping at you. You weren't the person who had upset me."

Sophia blinked. "You didn't snap at me."

He lifted a hand. "Yes, I did. And I apologize. I...I'm not having the best day."

Sophia made a tsking sound. "Reed Walker having a bad day? Is that even possible?"

He took another drag of his cigarette. "I'm allowed at least one, aren't I?" He tilted his head down and to the side to blow the tobacco away as if ashamed of smoking in front of her.

She smiled. "Well, you sure used yours to the max this morning."

His face clouded with regret.

She held up a hand as he opened his mouth. "Don't you dare apologize again. I know who you were directing your anger toward. And even if you *had* snapped at me, which you didn't, it was worth it to see Marcus get what's been coming to him. I think you just made yourself a legend around here. Today will be known as the day Reed Walker finally told off Marcus Weatherby." She shook her head. "I'll never forget the look on his face when you stood up and walked out on him. If

I'd had a camera, I would've taken that picture and framed it for my cubicle. And I'm still reeling over the fact that you dropped the f-bomb."

Reed smiled sadly. "I wonder if it'll get me fired."

Sophia shook her head. "No way. Kendrick will probably yell at Marcus for upsetting you." Her smile softened. "Besides, Marcus knows better than to try to get rid of you when Kendrick thinks you can do no wrong."

He winced. "He'll find out that's not so today, won't he?"

"Na. He'll be impressed your patience lasted this long." Sophia studied him for a moment, watching him look the file over before she decided to go straight to the heart of the matter. "But Marcus isn't the one you're really upset with, is he?"

His head came up. "What do you mean? I don't have difficulty with anyone else. I think we have a great team. Marcus is the only truly lazy—"

"I'm not talking about work." Her head tilted to one side as sympathy filled her. "What's wrong, Reed?"

His face drained of color. For a moment, she thought he might pass out. Then his eyelashes fluttered in a feminine way he managed to make look drop dead sexy and purely male. Finally, he gave the soft answer, "Nothing's wrong."

She exhaled a sad sigh. "You look like you've lost your best friend."

He glanced up, and his expression told her she'd guessed correctly. But instead of admitting anything, he lifted his cigarette. After tapping the end against the lip of the ashtray and setting the whole stick in a resting nook, his fingers fell limply to the table. Sophia slid her hand across the laminated surface and covered his. His knuckles were warm but they shook slightly under her palm.

"Why did you rush out of here on Friday?" she said in her softest, most concerned voice. "Why have you been gone the past few days? Why'd you show up late today?"

No answer.

"You're not wearing a tie."

He touched his throat and patted the area as if he hadn't realized he was without.

She blew out a quiet breath. "What happened to you, Reed?"

He stared at her for a long moment, looking as though he might spill everything. He even inhaled and opened his mouth. His lips moved, but no words came. Then he shook his head and slipped his hand out from under hers. After picking up his cigarette, he stabbed out the glowing tip.

Sophia sat back. "I know it's probably none of my business—"

"It's not," he interjected and just as quickly winced. "I'm sorry. I didn't mean to sound rude."

"No, don't be sorry. I'm the rude one, butting my nose into your personal life. But I'm concerned."

"I can't...I'm not..." He laughed at himself and looked away. "It's not something I can discuss."

"But I won't tell anyone." She sent him an encouraging smile. "I'm not the type to gossip."

One corner of his mouth quirked. "I know that."

"I just want to help if I can. You looked like you need a friend."

"I do." He instantly flushed as if he regretted saying that. Rubbing his eyes sockets, he sighed. "I know this sounds grade-schoolish, but...would you believe me if I said I'm sworn to secrecy?"

She studied him a moment before answering. "Yes, I would believe you." Then she grinned and leaned forward. "Am I free to guess, though?"

This time, both corners of his mouth tilted up. And her stomach turned over. Wow. She loved it when he smiled. A bit crooked and totally genuine, his grin was shy and boyishly adorable. It totally smothered the conservative restraint usually plastered across his features.

"Knock yourself out," he murmured. "But I still can't tell you if you guess correctly."

Sophia lifted her eyebrows. Was that a challenge? She

rubbed her hands together. "Excellent. I love a good puzzle." She scratched her chin with a perfectly manicured nail. "Let's see, let's see. What's the worst thing that could happen?" She snapped her fingers. "I've got it. You caught your woman with another man."

His eyebrows lofted in surprise. "No."

"You caught her with another woman?"

He looked shocked she'd even suggest such a thing. But he recovered quickly and shook his head. "No."

Trying to smother her smile, she said, "Did she catch *you?*"

Swinging his head back and forth, he blinked repeatedly, looking utterly perplexed. "I don't even have a girlfriend."

His quiet voice rattled her. She stopped breathing, unable to believe such a handsome, successful man wasn't taken. Then she sighed wistfully.

If only.

"Well that wiped out half of my guesses," she grumbled, straightening and finally able to ignore the little thrill dancing through her abdomen. Reed Walker was fair game. "It's not women trouble at all?" she asked, hoping she didn't sound too hopeful.

He gave her a look that clearly said no.

Thank God. "Do you have children?"

He shook his head.

"Okay." She bit the inside of her lip, feeling euphoric that he was truly, honestly available. "How about…Your dad has health problems? It's something really embarrassing you don't want anyone to know about, like some kind of STD maybe."

He shrugged. "I have no idea. I've never met the man before in my life. I couldn't even tell you his name."

Sophia's eyes widened; she sucked in a lungful. Whoops, way to go, idiot. He was already down about whatever. And here she was, throwing salt on an open wound, reminding him of his fatherless status.

Trying to ease up on him, she decided to go silly. "Your pet fish ran away?"

He rolled his eyes and, yes, his lips did that sexy crooked-smiling thing again. "Now you're reaching."

She grimaced, though inside, she beamed. "You're right. I am."

At that moment, two women walked into the break room. They took one look at Reed and scampered back out. Reed cleared his throat as if he realized he'd been doing something forbidden. "I have to finish reviewing this." He pushed to his feet and scooped up the file. "Or Marcus will have my ass. And, personally, I don't want him anywhere near that part of my anatomy."

Sophia sputtered out a surprised laugh. She couldn't believe how personable he was. Wow. Get to know the guy a little, and he was a freaking delight.

Rolling with the playful mood they had going, she feigned an exaggerated pout and sulked. "Fine then. I'll put my guessing game on hold." She stood and pointed a finger at him. "But I'm not finished with you yet, mister. Now sit. Finish your break. *I'll* go."

When she stepped out of the break room, a crowd had gathered. Most of them turned away and looked occupied when she appeared, but one noisy woman asked directly, "So what'd he say? Is he quitting?"

She frowned. "Reed? No. Why would he quit?"

"They say he lost it in the meeting today. Like he was sick of working here."

Anger sparked.

Sophia set her hands on her hips and glared. "He's having a bad day." Her eyes narrowed even more until the woman shied away. "Is it all right with you if the man has a bad day?"

The employee scowled and turned to bustle off. Sophia looked back toward the break room, where a few people were peeking inside.

Looking at the freak.

She wanted to snarl and chase them off. Everyone acted as if he wasn't to be talked to, but about. They treated Reed as if he was untouchable.

Okay, yes, there was something about him that set him

apart from everyone else. He didn't small talk and goof off but was all business during hours.

Sophia sniffed.

But he was just a man, a man who needed a friend. And she was determined to be one for him.

CHAPTER 8

Danni's bruises had healed by the morning she and Reed left his apartment to go to the doctor's office for her one-month checkup. It was her first trip outside since the attack. He worried how she'd handle the outside world again, and rightly so.

Sticking close to him, she bumped into his elbow every time he turned slightly or shifted directions. She glanced at him with apology in her expression. But it didn't bother him. He slung his arm around her shoulder and hauled her tight against him until she curled into his side with a relieved sigh.

He sat in the waiting room while she was examined. He glanced at the others around him. Closest to him, a mother rocked a sick, coughing child on her lap. Across the way, an elderly woman pulled out the contents of her purse and then put them all back in only to start rummaging again. An unshaven man quietly talked to himself in the corner. Reed stared at his hands for a moment and then picked up a magazine, blindly flipping through the pages.

When the nurse called him back, he popped to his feet and hurried after her. They found Danni in a room much like the one she'd been in before, sitting in exactly the same hunched over position, but this time without the blanket. The déjà vu that washed over him hit him full force in the solar plexus, and he could only stand there, staring.

Remembering.

The doctor ignored him, flipping through a clipboard. When he finally glanced up from under bushy gray brows, Reed stepped inside.

"Hello, Mr. Walker."

Reed went to Danni's side and stood close enough for her to lean against him if she needed to. She didn't

"Well, your sister is definitely not pregnant," the doctor started.

Alarmed to hear that news, Reed blinked. He hadn't even thought about her getting—

The very possibility made him suddenly queasy. Oh, God. She could've gotten pregnant after all that.

"And it seems that she's healing nicely," the doctor continued. "I did give her something to help slow the bleeding. But that should stop on its own soon enough."

Reed nodded and glanced down at Danni. *What bleeding?* Her head was lowered so she couldn't read the question in his eyes.

"The cast can come off in another two weeks." The doctor flipped all the pages back down. "We detected no sexually transmitted diseases and no infections, so after the cast is removed, I see no reason why she'll have to come back, except in a year or so, just for precautions."

Reed blew out a breath. "Thank you."

As the doctor left, Reed studied the top of Danni's head. She wore it in a ponytail again, but it wasn't as high as it used to be. Now, she tied her hair at the base of her neck like a tired old woman.

"Ready?" he asked.

She nodded and slid off the patient examining table.

As they walked the three blocks back to his car, she huddled so close to him her arm pressed into the side of his ribs. He pulled her back under his arm and talked quietly in her ear to soothe her. He didn't know what to say but he babbled on anyway, incessantly rambling about the weather and what he'd make them for supper until they made it to his Lexus.

When they reached his apartment, Danni looked exhausted. Dark smudges underlined her eyes, showing how frayed her nerves were. He hated how she jumped at every sound.

"Why don't you lie down? It's been a long morning."

When she nodded without complaint and went into his room, he closed his eyes. Then he climbed out onto the fire escape and stood with his hands in his pockets while he kept his lips firmly clamped around a cigarette. The wind was brisk and chilly. He turned his collar up so the cool air couldn't slither down his jacket. The clouds were thick and hung low over the earth, hovering like an overprotective mother bird shadowing her young under her wing.

Reed wanted to go back to the office. He could still get half a day's work in. He could bury himself in numbers and accounts and not come out until quitting time. But Danni had been through a rough morning, being prodded and poked, and made to answer uncomfortable questions. He felt guilty for even *wanting* to escape.

What had the doctor meant by bleeding? Was it internal or vaginal? Did she still have pain? Reed knew nothing about what was happening to his sister. God, what she must be going through. He crushed the tip of his cigarette, tucked the butt away, and had to have one more before going in.

When he climbed through the window, he checked on her. She was still asleep, only her arm in the cast and her head poked out above the covers. He nudged her awake and said he was going to be gone for a little while and to call his cell phone if she needed anything. She nodded, murmured something, and closed her eyes once more.

~ * ~

Since the police had given him the go-ahead, Reed went to

Danni's dorm room.

If he was going stir-crazy at his place with nothing to do, what must she be going through? He could escape to work every day and forget their problems for a few hours. But she had nothing to help her deal. All she had was his television, computer, and her own thoughts.

Reed wondered if she wanted to get back to work. He checked her mail slot before going up to her room. The box was almost crammed full. He tucked her letters under his arm and took the stairs up. In the hallway, he felt a sudden anxiety.

A tension worked between his shoulder blades. This was where her attacker had stood. He'd planned far enough ahead to bring gloves and a mask. He'd waited right here to pounce.

Reed unlocked her door and could almost feel it being ripped out of Danni's grasp as her assailant would've done when he forced it open. It would've swung so fast that the handle put a hole in the wall. Reed could already hear her scream of fear.

His body shuddered as the door slowly fell open. He could not go inside. He covered his nose with his sleeve and gagged.

"God almighty," he gasped, and stumbled back.

He leaned against the opposite wall and tried to catch his breath as he gaped at the door that was still slightly ajar.

What was that smell? He didn't even want to guess.

He took a deep breath and then forced his way in.

He cleaned the mess, wiping up blood and feces.

He had to use the bathroom once to vomit, but other than that, he got the walls and floor scrubbed. He swept up the glass and righted the table.

By the time, he finished, he felt ill all over again.

Gathering some clothes and personal effects, Reed listened to Danni's messages on her answering machine, jotted them down, then packed her sketching and painting supplies. He couldn't remember a time when she was without a sketchpad of some kind. Sometimes she'd just doodle on a napkin if that was all that was available. But Reed hadn't seen her draw one thing since the attack.

He hoped her supplies would help. He wanted his Danni back. He wanted the agony to go away. He wanted the guilt at not being there for her to disappear. He'd do anything to bring her around. But he couldn't push.

For some reason, a picture of Sophia Eschell floated through his mind. The only moment he'd felt halfway human lately was when he'd sat in the break room at Kendrick with her, and she'd flirted with him, turning silly with her guessing game. God, she'd even managed to make him smile.

He wanted to smile again. He wanted to repress the pain and memories and move on with his life. But that seemed so impossible to obtain.

When he returned home, Danni was in the kitchen. She had pasta boiling and reported that Nic had been home and gone again. Reed set her supplies on the counter, telling her he'd picked up a couple of her things.

Danni gave them a brief look, then turned away. "Thank you," she said, but did not seem excited to see them.

~ * ~

Sophia had never studied the back of a man's head before. But as she entered the records room at Kendrick and found Reed in front of a filing cabinet, riffling through the top drawer, her eyes fell to the back of his neck.

He had a nice neck. Not too thick, not too thin. It seemed sturdy and durable as it supported his head, which was tilted down as he examined the names on each file. Reed usually kept his hair short and neat. But it was starting to grow small black curls along each side under his ears.

Lately, she found herself always scanning the office for him. After the scandal he'd caused in the meeting room, he was still a hot topic in the gossip circles, so all she had to do was keep one ear open, and she usually knew right where he was.

It made her furious that instead of seeing if they could help him in any way, her coworkers had opted to point and whisper behind his back.

Well, not her.

Reed Walker was a nice guy and the pillar of this department. She wasn't going to stand aside and watch him crumble. She was going to support him however she could. She hated seeing something bad come of a good man, especially a good man who made her body jolt alive with intense awareness, which reminded her he had a nice tush to match the nice shape of the back of his head.

As she slipped into the records room behind him, her gaze traveled up his suit jacket. The man had an excellent form all the way around. She'd compliment his tailor if she knew who was responsible for the way his blazer molded to his wide shoulders and tapered waistline. She had to appreciate everything about his looks. And as she did, she frowned.

Reed had always been an attractive man, but lately she'd felt an extra something when she looked at him. A jump in the stomach, a sudden catch in her breath. It felt like hope, as if she actually might stand a chance with him after all.

It better not be sympathy. Sophia refused to once again need a wounded man to nurture back to health. Never, ever again.

Oh, God, could it be her Florence Nightingale syndrome acting up? Was weakness and neediness in a man always going to attract her? Was Myrna right, was she nothing but a magnet for troubled guys?

She shook her head. No, no. She'd just noticed Reed more lately because she wanted to help him, and in noticing, she'd realized how attainable he actually was.

Determined to ignore the blossoming attraction and just be a friend, she strolled forward. He didn't notice her until she sidled next to him. Sophia crossed her arms over the top of the filing cabinet and rested her chin on them.

He frowned and looked up. When he saw it was her, his eyebrows rose. Sophia loved that instant when his gaze first met hers, the initial spark in his eyes when she watched him focus and recognize. His attraction set her nerve endings on fire. But he always ruined it, clouding the look over with distant courtesy.

Sophia watched his eyes clear. "Hey," he murmured.

"Hey, yourself." She ignored the ball of disappointment and grinned mischievously. "Rumor has it that one Mr. Reed Walker did not show up for work again yesterday. He called in sick. Now according to calculations, that is five times in one month. It's a record, you know. I read it in the gossip column."

He watched her for a second, then his eyes fell, and his attention dropped back to studying the files. "And here I thought all gossip was a lie."

She examined the top of his head. It was obvious he didn't have professional work done aside from a quick trim, but his black locks still fell stylishly and framed his face perfectly.

"Of course, it's also being said the reason you took off was because you had an interview with the Delta Advertising firm."

Reed smiled. "Did I? You know, I *do* know a guy there. Think they'll hire me?"

Sophia's eyes followed the sure, steady movement of his fingers as he flipped past more folder tabs. "I definitely wouldn't use Kendrick as a reference if you do try to go elsewhere."

"Hmm," was his only reply.

He paused, pulled up a file and opened it. Sophia watched him shuffle through a few pages. It couldn't be work that bugged him. He didn't seem concerned about his job at all. And there was no way he'd applied somewhere else. He wouldn't act so invested in that dossier in his hand if he had.

She was so busy thinking up more guesses to his problem that what she said next shocked even her. "Do you want to have lunch with me?"

His head jerked up, the report in his hand instantly forgotten. She had to hold in a smug smile. Well that got his attention.

Then she sucked in her breath. What was she *doing*? She'd just asked the senior accountant to lunch.

"What?" His voice sounded winded.

Quickly, she tried to rationalize her rash behavior. If he

asked why, she'd say she wanted more time to guess his problem. And that was the truth. Mostly. Maybe if she got him outside the office and into a less business-oriented area, he'd be more willing to let her help him as a friend.

She lifted her eyebrows. *Keep it cool, Sophia.* "Have you eaten already?"

He checked his watch as if that held the answer. "No."

"Do you like the menu at Houston's?"

He frowned. "I guess."

"So?" She had to smile. He was so cute when he was flabbergasted.

But he was going to say no. She knew the answer would be no. His mouth opened and his tongue touched the roof of his mouth, forming a *no*. In the panic of being shot down, she took her hands off the file cabinet and prepared to retreat, when he suddenly answered, "Okay."

CHAPTER 9

"Is it illegal?"

Reed glanced up. "Pardon?"

Sophia walked beside him down a crowded sidewalk toward the restaurant located another block ahead of them. He still couldn't believe he was having lunch with her, or that she'd even been the one to ask. He tried not to gawk. But she kept spitting questions at him, and when he made eye contact, he got lost.

"This big mystery that's troubling you," she clarified. "It's not illegal, is it?"

His lips quirked with amusement. The lady was certainly persistent. "What do you think?"

If Danni hadn't begged him to keep it quiet, he would've told Sophia the truth by now. It wasn't something to blab to the whole department. But like she'd already mentioned, she wasn't a gossip, and she was just trying to help. On the other hand, he'd probably end up crying all over her if he tried to explain the situation. Not the manliest thing to do to the girl of your dreams during your first lunch together.

Sophia tapped her chin with a long fingernail as she studied him, and he almost sighed. Those nails were going to drive him mad. They shouldn't be legal. He couldn't stop wondering how they'd delight him if they ever slid over his skin.

"No. It's not illegal," she finally decided.

He looked down at his feet. "I guess I'm relieved you don't think I'm a criminal. And yet a little disappointed you think I'm so boring."

She laughed. "Oh, you're not boring."

Reed's instinct to mate went into overdrive, but he pushed the craving down and barely touched the base of her back as he opened the door to Houston's.

Letting her precede him inside, he inhaled her fragrance as she brushed past. Her mind-drugging perfume stuck in his nose and made his yearning for her even harder to reign in.

Sophia was taller than any of the other women he'd ever been interested in. But that brought her face closer and her smell closer. All she had to do was tilt her chin up, and their mouths would be aligned perfectly for a kiss.

Maybe she could kiss all his pain away.

He had to stop for a moment and catch his sanity while she strolled to the greeter and ordered a table for two. His gaze fell to her legs as she moved. She wore a mid-length skirt that hugged her curves and showed off her trim ankles and calves. It was a conservative outfit, but it heightened his curiosity, which was pretty high in the first place.

Feeling antsy, he unconsciously tugged his pack of cigarettes from his jacket's pocket.

"A table for two," the *maître d'* repeated, glancing at Reed's cigarettes. "Smoking or non?"

Just as Sophia said, "Non," Reed answered, "Smoking."

The man paused with a frown, and Reed's gaze collided with Sophia's.

She managed a sheepish grin. "Right, I forgot."

Reed slipped his pack back in his pocket and wanted to say non-smoking was fine. But he needed a fix. Now. He lowered his head a fraction. "Sorry."

The *maître d'* continued to wait for an answer. Sophia sent him a smile. "Smoking, please," she corrected.

Since it was earlier than the normal lunch hour, they were immediately led to an outside table, where the weather was chilly but thankfully warmer than it had been lately. Still, they both left their coats on. As they waited for drinks and then the meal, she threw out a few more guesses, but he could tell she was mostly just teasing.

He'd just taken a bite into his chicken salad when she mused, "You're a very private man, Reed Walker."

He chewed thoughtfully. After swallowing, he asked, "What do you want to know about me?"

"Everything." She leaned forward with a gleam in her eye. "But mostly whatever is bugging you?"

His gaze dropped as he swirled his fork between the lettuce leaflets until he found another piece of chicken.

Sophia sighed and leaned back. "Okay, fine. Tell me about your family then."

He suddenly wished he'd never roused her curiosity. It was pure heaven sitting with her, sharing a cozy little table in the corner, a bit secluded from everyone else. But he really was a private man. He didn't want to explain his family.

"I, uh, I have a sister. And a roommate."

"A sister and a roommate." She repeated before her eyes went huge and she slapped both hands over her mouth, muffling out the words, "*Roommate!* I didn't even think of that."

He frowned, totally clueless. "Think of what?"

Her face flushed a bright red; he'd never seen anyone blush so furiously. After knocking back a large gulp of her iced tea, she madly fanned at her cheeks. "I'm so sorry, Reed. I feel like a complete idiot. I've never been good at being able to tell the difference between—" She broke off to press her hands to the sides of her scarlet cheeks.

He squinted. "You've never been good at being able to tell the difference between *what?*"

Ignoring him, she continued her mortified rant, "And all that time in the break room, I kept accusing you of *woman* trouble. You should've just stopped me then and corrected me. I hope I didn't insult you."

He stopped her now. "Wait. I'm lost. What're we talking about?"

She froze and dropped her hands. "Your roommate."

"Okay." He arched a brow, not catching on. "What about him?"

She stared, speechless, until it finally struck him.

"Oh!" The breath rushed from his lungs. Wow, the woman of his dreams thought he preferred men, which wouldn't have bothered him...if he'd been gay.

Insulted, horrified, and just plain heartbroken, he felt his own face heat. "No," he croaked. This could not be happening.

Sophia closed her eyes. "Oh, my God," she whispered. "I did it again, didn't I? I'm so sorry. When you said roommate, I thought—"

"No," he repeated. "He's just...a roommate. A *roommate*, roommate. Totally platonic."

Nic, the bastard, would probably get a kick out of this. He'd play it up and insist he was the male part of the couple. But Reed couldn't be so blasé.

Sophia opened her lashes and winced. "Okay," she spoke loudly, her eyes glassy with humiliation and her color still high. "Now that I've stuck my foot into my mouth twice in a row, we should be good for the rest of the meal. But, oh Lordy. I'm so sorry, Reed."

"It's okay," he assured, still too damn uncomfortable for words. But Christ. The one woman he wanted to be with most in the world actually thought he was gay. "I guess it does sound strange for two grown men to share an apartment together, though in our defense, we bought it straight out of college when we were both still penniless. Then we put so much work into it, fixing it up. Now we're just waiting for the other to move out first."

Sophia smiled, the tension in her shoulders relaxing. Some of the strain in the air eased as well. "So, a sister and a roommate, huh?" she said, sending him a bright, forced grin. "Sounds like a huge family."

He shrugged, clearing his throat. "It saves at Christmas."

She threw her head back and laughed, and from there, everything was good again. Reed's breath caught at the sight of her chuckling. God, could she be any more gorgeous?

"I imagine it does. I, on the other hand, am overwhelmed at Christmas. I have three grandparents still alive, both my parents, a brother, who has a wife and two kids. Then three sisters, all married with children." She rolled her eyes. "Not to mention cousins and aunts and uncles galore."

Listening to her, Reed stopped eating to stare. She really did have a huge family. His heart ached at the thought of aunts and uncles. Grandparents.

He wondered where his mother's parents might be. Joan had never talked about her relatives. Reed marveled over the wonder of a family tree. He suddenly felt like an orphan. His roots began with him and Danni. Yet Sophia could name people back to the country they'd emigrated from. He fell a little bit more in love with her as he watched her smile fondly as she spoke.

"...and being the baby of the family was no fun either. My brother, Deke, could be a real terror sometimes." She shrugged, giving him a slight smile. "Actually, we're pretty average. Nothing fancy."

Reed wanted to argue. She had everything he'd ever dreamed of—a nice, close-knit, average family. But instead of going on a tirade about how lucky she was, he merely asked, "Is your family from here?"

"Nah. My mom's side is from South Carolina, and Dad's...well, I'm not quite sure where they're from. I'm a lot closer to the Atchett side."

He frowned. "Why is that?"

"My dad came from a broken home. He left them when he was seventeen, and I don't think he's talked to any of them since."

Sophia paused, looking thoughtful. "You know, now that I think of it, all the women I'm related to have gone for guys from dysfunctional families."

Reed's eyebrows rose. *Really?*

"It all started with my Grandma Atchett." She paused and frowned. "No, I guess it started with her mom. She married a guy whose father refused to claim him, so he got into a lot of fights when he was little. And then my Grandma Atchett first met Grandpa when he had a black eye from when his dad punched him. And then her daughter, my mom, met my dad right before he decided to run away from home. Dad grew up in Raytown, you see, and he never knew his father. Grandma Atchett was a child psychologist, and she was my dad's psychologist. Then, later, *he* became a psychologist. Then my sisters, of course, found men from divorced parents and the like.

"Anyway, to say the least, my females in my family have been irresistibly drawn to guys with bad pasts." She grinned at Reed. "And I have this awful premonition the gene was passed down to me too. So don't go telling me that you had a rough upbringing or I'll probably just fall in love with you on the spot."

Reed's chest felt suddenly tight. He didn't dare to dream about the possibility of Sophia Eschell falling in love with him. But God, he suddenly felt too hopeful to be rational.

"I guess I'll just keep all my skeletons in the closet then."

Sophia chuckled, the low sound heading straight to his lap. She folded her hands and set her chin on them as she studied him with a pair of big brown eyes he wanted to drown in.

"I'll say one thing for you. If, by chance, you did have a misspent youth, then you did an excellent job of pulling yourself up by the bootstraps."

Suddenly not liking how perceptive this woman was, Reed lowered his face and focused on eating. When he glanced her way again, she was watching him with those all-seeing brown eyes of hers.

"How's your meal?" he asked, needing a change of topic.

She shrugged. "It's okay. But I was kind of in the mood for Italian."

"Oh?" He frowned. "Then why didn't you order—"

"Stop right there," Sophia said, holding up her hand. "I can explain."

At Reed's blank look, she laughed again.

"My dad and I created this really good red sauce. We call it the rhyming Eschell Special. It's so good I can't bear to eat Italian food that wasn't cooked by him or me."

Reed nodded to her plate of half-eaten sweet and sour pork. "So that's why you're eating Chinese?"

"You betcha." She sat back, her eyes glittering. "Any Italian restaurant I try only comes up second best."

Reed leaned in across the table. "Well, now I gotta know what's in the sauce."

She smiled devilishly and shook her long-nailed finger at his nose. "No way. Family secret. But I can tell you I make a mean spaghetti and lasagna and manicotti and—" She paused suddenly and gave him a slight frown. "Hey, how did we get on to the topic of me and my family? I thought we were talking about yours."

Reed took a drink of his water. "I thought we did," he said as he set the glass down.

She gave him a look that clearly said they hadn't even scratched the surface. As she picked at a piece of sweet and sour pork, she said, "A sister and a roommate, huh? What's your sister's name?"

A muscle in Reed's jaw jerked. "Danielle," he said quietly. "But I call her Danni."

Just saying her name made everything come back. He ditched his meal and dug out his cigarettes. His eyes jerked up when Sophia made a startled sound.

"Danielle? You mean Danielle *Walker*?"

Reed nodded. His hands stilled in the middle of pulling out a cigarette. "Do you know her?"

Sophia shook her head. "*Know her*? I wish. Your sister is truly Danielle Walker? Danielle Walker, the author?"

Reed glanced down at his cigarettes. "She writes and illustrates children's books, yeah."

Sophia gasped and suddenly pressed a hand to her heart. "Oh my God. You're Danielle Walker's brother. I can't believe I didn't know that. I *love* her stories." Reed frowned as she rushed on. "I read them to my nieces and nephews when I baby-sit. Her stories are just adorable. The things she comes up with to write about. And the pictures are so fun. I just...I can't believe you're her brother. That's so amazing. I knew she was a local author, but still...wow."

Reed stared, a little amused. He never knew the sophisticated Sophia Eschell could turn into such a fanatic. It was fascinating. "I could probably get you an autograph if you want."

Her mouth fell open. "Could you? Ohmigod!" Then she straightened. "I mean, you don't have to do that." But she leaned forward, her eyes ablaze. "Actually, I'd love for my niece, Layla, to meet her. She really gets a kick out of your sister's books."

Reed fell back in his seat. "Sure. I think Danni would do that." Someday she would. Hopefully. "She loves kids." At least she used to.

"Wow." Sophia repeated, all smiles. "Thank you." She continued talking, describing the books of Danni's that she liked the best. "And I heard she was, like, really young when she published her first book."

Reed smiled sadly. "She was sixteen." He and Danni had broken the law a little in that regard. Her publishers still believed he was her father who'd signed legal guardianship consent for her until she'd become an adult. She'd spit out six picture book stories before she'd been able to legally sign her own contract.

He hoped Danni would be able to do so again, that she'd be able to live again soon.

He studied Sophia with her glittering, excited eyes and wanted to feel as animated as she looked. He wanted to soak in her joy and her smiles. But there was something in him that felt dead.

If only something could bring him back to life.

CHAPTER 10

It was almost two in the morning when Nic entered his apartment building with a clinging blonde attached to him. He'd wanted to go back to her house but was surprised to discover she had two sleeping kids and a babysitter there. He'd debated a hotel room, but Rhonda wanted to know what was wrong with his place.

"My roommate's sister is staying with us for a while."

"So? She's better than a three and seven-year-old listening in on us."

Nic ground his teeth and was about to argue when she slipped her hand over a very coaxing area of his anatomy.

"Okay," he said, and closed his eyes. "But we have to be quiet."

She laughed against his collarbone. "Are you sure you *want* me to be quiet?"

He groaned, figuring he was probably doomed, but threw caution to the wind and ushered her toward the elevator anyway.

By the time they made it to his apartment, he wasn't thinking with his brain at all. He opened the door and took her hand.

"Shh," he said into her ear as he led her toward his room through the dark kitchen.

"Why don't you turn the light on," she asked.

"Shh!" He stopped. "My roommate's on the couch." He could hear Reed's deep breathing. He slid off his shoes and urged Rhonda to do the same. She giggled as they tip-toed by the sofa.

"Shh," Nic hissed yet again.

She smothered the noise with her hand. "It's like we're trying to sneak past your parents or something."

Yeah, well, Reed discovering him with company—of the female variety—would probably be worse than his parents discovering them.

Nic pulled her into his room and as the door quietly clicked shut behind them, he pushed her onto his bed and followed her down. Her fingers were quick to unbutton his shirt, where they dipped inside the opened cloth, sliding over his chest. She tried to pull the garment off, but the sleeves caught at the cuffs.

Nic made a sound deep in his throat and buried his face in her neck where her hair spread over his pillow. This was going to be good.

Oh, God. So good.

~*~

Noises from just outside her room interrupted her sleep. Feet shuffled by the door. Mumbled words were spoken. She listened to them move into another room. Some kind of scuffling followed and then the loud squeak of bedsprings.

Then, "Oh! Stop. *Stop!*"

"Shh."

The room was shrouded in black when Danni's eyes flew open. She wasn't completely awake yet but stuck somewhere between semi-consciousness and nightmare. The comforter had fallen down to her waist, leaving her chilled.

In the other room, something crashed to the floor.

She sprang out of bed. Her heartbeat accelerated to an alarming speed. The air rushed from her lungs.

It was happening again. No, not again. To someone else. She glanced around the room. The light from a streetlamp outside helped her grow accustomed to the dark. Spinning in a circle, she looked for a weapon. She needed protection.

That's when she saw it. The bat in the corner seemed to glow. The way the window was positioned, it looked as if the bat were spotlighted there, knowing she needed it.

She rushed by, grabbing it as she went, and dashed out of the room, still not completely awake to rationalize what was really happening.

~*~

Nic had already wiggled Rhonda out of a couple articles of clothing when he decided he needed to see what lay underneath. He reached over and groped for the light, accidentally knocking a few things to the floor. After a wince, hoping the noise hadn't woken anyone, he fumbled some more.

"Hurry," the voice under him demanded.

"Just a sec," he hissed. His fingers found the string that dangled from his bedside lamp. He tugged and a soft glow filtered through the room.

He sat up to look his fill. Her shirt lay crumpled somewhere on the floor, her bra dangled from a nearby chair, but her face did not hold the excited, glossy-eyed expression he'd expected. Instead, a look of complete horror marred her features as she gawked behind him.

Nic frowned and started to turn. But as he twisted, the bat swung.

It missed him by a scant millimeter. He felt the air whoosh past his cheek. Startled, he fell back and landed on Rhonda, who screamed and left his right ear ringing.

"Whoa," he yelped, gawking up at the bat-wielding figure.

His eyes went wide as they focused on Danni. Her hair was

a mess, tangled and frizzed into a frightening ball of chaos. Her eyes were wild, glassed over with fear. She wore a long-sleeved flannel top with an array of teddy bears printed on the cloth and pants to match.

She raised the bat again with one hand, while the other remained wrapped in a cast.

"Get off me," Rhonda screamed under him.

"Get off her!" Danni repeated. "Get away from her."

Immediately, Nic rolled off Rhonda and onto the floor. He landed on all fours and looked up just in time to see Reed dash into the room.

"Danni!" He grabbed her from behind, wrapping his arms around her waist and pulling her away from Rhonda and Nic.

Rhonda yanked a blanket up to cover herself. Nic remained shirtless as he lurched to his feet and raised both hands.

"It's okay," he panted out. "Everything's fine, Danni. I wasn't hurting her. Rhonda?" He glanced at the blonde, who ogled Danni as if she were the murderer in a horror flick. "*Rhonda*," he repeated until she looked at him. "Tell Danni you're okay."

Rhonda's mouth fell open. "The hell if I am." She dropped his sheet long enough to grab a shirt off the floor and pull it on. It was bulky on her and had the letters K-State stenciled across the chest. "This is crazy. I'm so out of here."

"Rhonda." Nic's rushed after her as she scurried around to collect her scattered apparel and flee from his room.

~*~

Reed gently shook the bat out of Danni's hand.

In the living room, he heard Nic trying to explain things to his date without revealing Danni's secret. "I told you my roommate and his sister were here."

"Well you forget to mention the woman was a bat-wielding nutcase."

"She's *not* a nutcase."

"She's frigging loony, Nic."

In Nic's room, Danni met Reed's gaze, realization and horror dawning in her expression. "I messed up, didn't I?"

Through the apartment, they heard, "Don't call me again."

"Wait a second. That's—" But the door had already slammed. "That's my favorite shirt," Nic finished, crestfallen.

He turned away and threw his hand in the air. "Wonderful. Thanks a lot, Danni."

Reed and Danni paused in the doorway to his room. Danni huddled under Reed's arm as the bat dangled limply from his free hand. When Nic fisted his hands onto his hips and scowled, Danni shrank farther into Reed.

"I'm so sorry, Nic."

Nic gave a short bark of laughter. "Sorry? What did you think I was doing to her? Did you actually believe I was hurting her? How could you think that about me? I'm not going to do to some girl what that guy did to you."

Tears filled her eyes.

Nic threw his head back and sighed. "How long have you known me, Danni?"

"Don't," Reed growled.

Danni buried her head into his shoulder. "I wasn't thinking," she cried. "I'd just woken up, and I heard noises. Then I heard her say stop."

"Shh," Reed said, cuddling her close. "Don't feel bad about it. It's okay. You did *nothing* wrong."

Nic closed his eyes and rubbed his forehead. "I wasn't hurting her," he repeated. "I was...I was tickling her," he finished quietly, an embarrassed blush staining his cheeks.

"It doesn't matter what you were doing," Reed growled. "What were you *thinking*, bringing a woman here?"

Nic stopped rubbing and shot him a scowl. "You *know* what I was thinking."

"Yeah, with your dick instead of your head. Don't ever bring a woman around again while Danni's here."

"Excuse me? This is my home too."

"Frankly, I don't care who you screw, or when, or where," Reed growled. "As long as it's not here while Danni's in the next room."

"Don't tell me what—"

"Stop it!" With tears streaming down her face, Danni pulled away from Reed. "Just stop it. Both of you. It's my fault. I'm sorry." She covered her mouth with her hands. "I'm so sorry," she rasped in a small voice and spun around, dashing into Reed's room.

Both men stared after her until the door clicked shut. Then Nic whirled away and ran his hand through his hair, grumbling. "Great. Now I feel like a total douche."

"Good," Reed said. "Because you are." He followed Danni into his room.

"He didn't do anything wrong," Danni said as soon as he entered.

"He didn't do anything right either."

"You need to apologize to him. This is his home, not mine. He should be able to do...whatever he wants here."

"I'm not apologizing to that ass. He knew better than to—"

"Go," Danni said in a stern, authoritative voice that made Reed lift his brows.

This was the first sign of life from his sister in weeks. Relieved to see some of the old Danni coming back, he found himself quietly turning and following her orders out the door.

Nic was no longer in the living room. After checking his bedroom, Reed finally caught sight of his roommate through the window that led out onto the fire escape. Scowling, he started forward.

The cold wind caught his bare chest as he stuck his head out the window. He crawled outside anyway. Nic wasn't any more dressed than he was, and he refused to look like a pansy by going back in for a shirt.

The city was quiet. Cars passed by the opening of the alley on the street to the left, but the alley below them looked dead. Only a few cans and bottles stirred in the breeze

Nic sighed and ran his hands through his hair. "I borrowed your spot for a minute."

Reed stopped beside him. "Well, get out. I need it now."

Nic muttered under his breath then stuffed his hands in his pockets. "How's she doing?"

Reed picked up a cigarette from the pack he had lying on the ledge. He tried to light it but had to cup his hands around the flame before it caught. He waited to exhale before he answered. "She's feeling pretty bad. Told me to apologize to you."

Nic laughed. "Apologize? Why?"

"Because this is your home, too, and I had no right to tell you what you can and cannot do in it." Reed flicked some ashes over the side.

Nic watched the small embers fall and burn out before they reached the alley floor. "Hell, you were the one who was right. I shouldn't have brought Rhonda here. I wasn't...I just thought if we were really quiet, no one would wake up."

They were both silent before Nic said, "I'll apologize to her tomorrow."

"Good."

Another quiet minute followed. Both men huddled in the breeze with their arms crossed over their bare chests, staring out at the dark night.

Reed took another drag and then he quietly confessed, "I went to lunch with Sophia."

Nic's head spun around. "When?"

"Today."

Nic turned and leaned back against the rail, letting a slow smile spread across his cheeks. "So you finally got the nerve to ask her out, huh?"

"Nope. She asked me."

Nic cocked an eyebrow. "For business reasons?"

Reed went thoughtful before he answered. "I don't recall talking about the office at all."

Nic whooped. "Way to go, my man. So are you going out again?"

Reed shook his head. He let out a stream of smoke and watched the cloud whip away in the breeze. Nic's smile mellowed into a puzzled frown.

"What? Why not?"

Reed shrugged. "I felt guilty. When we were returning to work, I thought about Danni, and I couldn't say anything to Sophia about her. It just didn't seem right. I was out to lunch with the woman of my dreams, and Danni was sitting in there alone, miserable, in pain, and scared. I can't go out with Sophia. I can't feel things toward her and not be guilty. What kind of man would I be to go out and have a good time while my sister is alone and suffering. Besides, look how she reacted tonight to your date. I just can't...I can't do that to her."

Nic looked away. "If you're trying to make me feel awful for bringing Rhonda here and wanting to have a good time, it's working."

Reed lifted his face, surprised by his roommate's quiet tone. He hadn't even thought of his situations mirroring Nic's in any way. "That's not what I meant. Danni's not your sister. Not your responsibility."

"But—"

"Hey, I thought we were talking about me, you selfish ass. I'm trying to spill my guts about my dream woman, remember."

Nic flashed a quick grin. "So sorry," he murmured and fluttered out a hand, bowing slightly. "Please continue."

Reed frowned and flipped him off.

Nic's smile spread. "So Sophia's finally showing interest, but now you don't feel you can go out with her."

Reed eyeballed Nic a moment before glancing off into the night. "She knows something's wrong, says she wants to help, and I know she would. She's got a huge, caring heart. I have this feeling she'd take me in and make all the pain go away. But I swore to Danni I wouldn't tell anyone."

Nic listened quietly. Reed looked up to the sky, but the lights from the city blocked out most of the stars. There seemed to be nothing for him to wish upon.

"Well if this whole thing isn't one big mess." Nic let out a long sigh.

Reed could only nod. Would it ever end? Or could agony

be dragged out forever?

As they stood there and stared at the night, Reed dreamed of a way to solve his problems, having no clue of how to fix any of them. It all seemed so hopeless.

When he stubbed out his cigarette, his roommate slugged him on the back. "Let's go in. We've both got to get up early for work. And as they say, tomorrow is always another day."

CHAPTER 11

The next afternoon after work, Reed headed straight for the fire escape as soon as he entered his apartment. With a headache from Marcus piling more work on him, he needed a moment alone. By the time he climbed back inside and shut the window, his clothes reeked of smoke.

"Where's Danni?" he asked Nic, who sat in the corner of the living room at their computer desk, tapping a pen against the edge of the keyboard.

"In your room," he answered distractedly. "Said she needed a nap."

"Oh." Reed glanced toward the closed door of his bedroom, wondering if it'd ever really feel like *his* room again. He turned back to Nic. "What're *you* doing?"

Looking deep in thought as he scrolled through the screen on the computer, Nic frowned as he read. "Hmm?" He glanced up and blinked. "Oh. Nothing. Just...homework."

The two men had agreed not to discuss work since their companies were competitors. But it would've been incredibly easy to snoop into each other's secrets, since they saved information from each firm on their home computer. But of course, both Nic and Reed respected each other's privacy and wouldn't do such a thing.

Nic had the stereo on, playing low. He owned a huge selection of music, but Reed couldn't remember hearing this tune before. Idly, he picked up the CD case resting on the top of one of Nic's three-foot high speakers and read the cover. Tori Amos. He flipped it over to the back and read the song list. His eyebrows rising, he set the case back down. It wasn't the sort of thing Nic usually preferred, but he honestly did like a wide variety.

Reed started for the kitchen. Maybe he'd get a snack. But something resting on the corner of the couch caught his eye. He stopped and glanced down. It wasn't work that Nic had brought home from Delta Advertising. Reed picked up the pile of pamphlets and scanned briefly. His eyes rose to the desk, even though his head remained lowered.

"What is this?" he demanded in a cold, quiet voice.

Nic glanced up and was about to turn back to his computer screen, but paused. He stared at the sheets in Reed's hand. His mouth opened and then closed.

"It's just, ah, some homework I was doing."

"Why did you leave it lying *here?*"

Nic slipped to his feet and took a few steps toward Reed. But the look Reed sent him warned him not to come closer. He raised a hand and pointed at it. But the hand fell limply.

"Look. There's good information in there. I think Danni could get some use from it."

Reed lowered his gaze and read aloud, "The Rape, Abuse, and Incest National Network." He shook his head. "No," he snarled, and threw the pages back onto the couch. "No, Nic. She's not ready."

"Oh, come on, Reed. Would you just look through it? It says to encourage them to seek professional help. And Danni *needs* help. She tried to kill me last night."

But Reed wasn't listening. He stalked toward the kitchen, away from the discussion.

Nic followed. "It happened, Walker. It happened to Danni. Why are you pretending it didn't?"

Reed stopped and spun to face him. He raised his hand. "I don't want to talk about it."

"It's still going to be there." Nic stood his ground. Like a stern father, he gave Reed a steady look. "Go ahead and try to ignore it, but this isn't something that's just going to go away. She was raped. Someday, we're all going to have to face it and find a way to work through it, not *around* it."

Reed lowered his hand and sucked in a deep, stuttered breath. He shook his head and gave Nic a poignant look. The man knew next to nothing about how to deal with trauma. He'd never lived trauma. The biggest upset in his life had probably been waiting a full month to get that bicycle when he was nine.

"Don't act like you know how to fix this," he said. "You've never been hurt like she has. You...don't...know. So back off. Let me handle my sister my way. We just need time."

He turned and entered the kitchen. Nic let out a disgusted breath. "Why are you so afraid to get her some help?"

Apprehension prickled Reed's scalp as secrets flashed through him. If Danni sought help and told someone about all her problems, she'd have to talk about the past, and tell someone about *every* skeleton in their closet. And he liked his skeletons right where they were, thank you very much.

He spun to shoot Nic a glare. "I *am* helping her." Pointing a finger at the pamphlets on the couch, he hissed, "Don't you think the hospital shoved those things down her throat already? Trust me, she knows where to go when she's ready. And she's *not* ready. This is my sister, not yours. Can't you just look at her and see she wants to be left alone right now? Let her adjust."

Nic tilted his head. "Funny," he said with a short laugh. "When I look at her, I see a face that's begging for help."

Reed ran a hand through his hair. "Well, it's not your decision."

"Fine." Nic raised his hands in defeat and turned away. "Have it your way."

"Thank you," Reed said to Nic's retreating back, even

though he wasn't thankful at all. "And throw your *homework* away, would you? She's already got plenty of that crap to look at when it's time."

Nic jerked the papers off the couch and wadded them into a ball before slamming them into the trashcan. He slumped back to the computer just as the phone rang.

Reed picked up. "What?" he said testily.

"Reed?" the voice in the receiver asked uncertainly.

His breath caught in his throat. He'd know that voice anywhere. "Sophia?"

"Yeah." The smoky tone filled his ear and he closed his eyes briefly, drowning in the liquid lull of her voice. "Did I call at a bad time?"

~*~

Sophia bit her lip. Of course it was a bad time. She shouldn't have called.

"No," he was a little too quick to answer. "No. It's fine. I just...I was arguing with my roommate." He paused a moment. "I'm sorry. I didn't mean to snap..."

"Don't worry about it."

She closed her eyes and asked herself why she couldn't just leave him alone. She should stay away. He was going through some kind of personal crisis. That meant it was the worst time for him to get involved with anyone. He had "complicated" written all over him.

But she was strangely drawn to him. And he seemed so lost lately. Of course, that only enticed her more. Just like her mother and grandmother. She'd always been attracted to suffering men, which was yet another reason she should stay away.

"So," she said slowly, ignoring that persistent conscience of hers, screaming in her head, demanding she back off. "You win the argument?"

He laughed.

He actually laughed. It was music to Sophia's ears. Good.

The poor guy needed to laugh. He'd been looking way too serious and sad lately.

"So, what's up?"

Sophia paused at his question. He sounded so brief and gruff. She winced. Great, she shouldn't have called. He didn't want to talk to her.

Then, he quickly added, "I mean, was there some problem at work you need to discuss?"

Sophia bit her lip and knew she had an out. She should definitely say, *Sure, something's wrong at work, I need your advice*. She hadn't called because she couldn't get him out of her head. No way.

But she couldn't lie and therefore, she heard herself say, "Um, actually, no."

He paused. "Oh?"

What am I doing? What am I doing? Don't ask it, Sophia. Whatever you do, don't ask—

"I was wondering if you were busy Friday night. Or…" Her voice trailed off and it left a ringing tension in the air. "Or if you'd like to go to a film festival with me? They're featuring Marlon Brando movies. We could have our pick between *A Streetcar Named Desire*, *The Godfather* or *Apocalypse Now*. Or we could do a triple-header and take in all three."

~*~

There was a sudden pause, and Reed realized it was his turn to respond. The euphoria of hearing her ask him out was overwhelming. He just wanted to breathe it all in and sigh. But he couldn't. Reality reared its ugly head, butting away his dream. He scratched the back of his neck and found an interesting spot on the wall to study.

"*This* Friday?" He sucked in a loud breath. "I really can't this Friday."

"It's going on until Sunday," she put in helpfully.

Reed almost groaned. *Don't do this to me, Sophia*. He couldn't take much more. "Actually, the whole weekend's bad for me." He wanted to pound his head against the wall. He closed his eyes, wishing she wouldn't pressure him further, but dreading the possibility that she'd give up completely.

"Reed." Her voice sounded serious, as if she were talking to a young child and was trying to drag the truth from him. If she were right in front of him, she'd be looking at him levelly in the eyes. "Is that a can't or a won't? And be honest with me. If you just don't want to, that's perfectly fine. But I'd like to know so I can leave you alone."

No, don't leave me alone. He gritted his teeth. "It's a very nice idea, Sophia. And I'd love to go." He stopped talking, because he couldn't continue. Emotions clogged his throat. How could he have known that true agony would come from a five foot ten strawberry-blond that walked like temptation on heels?

"But..." she pressed.

He swallowed. "But right now isn't a good time."

"Okay," she said as if she understood, though her tone told clearly him she didn't. Reed didn't even understand. "Does this have to with the mysterious problem you're having?"

"Yes." He couldn't think of any reason why he should lie to her. Sophia deserved the truth even if he wasn't able to deliver all of it.

"Are you sure it isn't about a woman?"

His shoulders relaxed. "One hundred percent positive."

"Good. Because I'm going to get to you yet, Reed Walker. You just wait in see."

Reed glowed as she hung up. Someday.

He was still lost in the dizzying turn of events when Nic's voice came sharply from behind him.

"You've got to be the stupidest jackass I've ever met."

Reed turned, his dreamy mood evaporating.

Nic slowly shook his head. "Do you even realize what you just did? You didn't turn down some random woman. You turned down *the* woman of your dreams, Walker." He stared incredulously. "I have never seen you so crazy over one lady before. And you just...just told her no. What is wrong with you?"

"I have my reasons."

"I know your stupid reasons. And I think they're bullshit. If you actually believe it would bother Danni for you to go out with Sophia, then you have lost your freaking mind. She'd be happy for you, man. Just talk to her. I'm sure she wouldn't say no."

"I'm not going to leave Danni home alone while I…" He stopped and spun away, knowing it was useless to try explaining it to Nic.

"If Danni knew, she'd encourage you to go on this date."

Reed came back, his eyes blazing. "Don't even think about mentioning it to her. She doesn't need any kind of pressure or guilt right now."

"Fine." Nic turned back to his computer screen and muttered, "My lips are sealed…Moron."

CHAPTER 12

Copying machines had never induced her to want to commit murder before. But Sophia could taste that oh-so-vile concoction of pure frustration mix—or rather clash—with her own stubborn will as the one in front of her jammed.

Again.

For the fifth time.

Inappropriate words bubbled up her throat and threatened to spill out at any second.

Blowing at the stray hair that had wormed its way out of her tidy economical bun and was currently irritating the underside of her nose, she glanced up. The narrow slit in the wall that failed to prove itself as a worthy window teased Sophia with the slight glimpse of a busy city. Construction on the freeway below was the only hint of Kansas City she caught. It was probably for the best, because if the window were any bigger, she'd no doubt push the lousy copying machine right out its Plexiglas.

But instead of heaving at the large bulk with all her might, she took a deep breath and stuffed her head back into the stale nook where she'd been trying to release a crumpled sheet of jammed paper.

With barely any light to see worth a damn, she bent so far over she feared her new skirt might split open, right up the back seam. "Don't do this to me," she muttered.

The rustic piece of junk couldn't copy a simple memo if its mechanical little life depended on it. With a hard tug, she ripped the paper clean in half, leaving the other section still captured within relentless, motorized jaws. Holding the escaped remains, she straightened only to gawk down at the copy machine, her jaw coming loose and sagging a few inches to leave her mouth fallen open in pure dismay.

"You…you *monster*," she exploded, gritting her hands into fists stiffly down at her sides and glaring at the machine as she gave it a vicious kick with the tip of her high heel. "It took me an hour to fill out that stupid report. And this was the only freaking copy I had. Do you enjoy ruining my entire day? Jerk." She kicked it again. Which only managed to make her toes sting.

Actually it wasn't the copying machine that had ruined her day. Her morning had started off wrong when she'd woken with dried tears staining her pillow. She hadn't thought Reed turning her down when she'd invited him to the movies the afternoon before would hurt quite as much as it had. But as soon as she'd hung up with him, she'd burst into the weepies and hadn't been able to stop all evening.

To console herself, she stayed up late, watching tear-jerker romances on Netflix and clearing her entire apartment free of Kleenexes, chocolate, and double fudge ice cream.

Today, pain throbbed behind her eyes. Chocolate and tears always did that to her the day after a nasty binge. The choc-o-tears hangover she liked to call it, except maybe she should rename it the feeling-sorry-for-myself hangover.

Mentally counting to ten, she blew out a breath and bent again. The fabric of her skirt stretched once more, but she ignored it for the moment and wormed her fingers into the dark cranny, feeling for bits of paper. After her grasp slipped twice and she only came away with a one inch by one inch scrap of document, she growled. "Bastard! That's it. You're going down."

She had no idea how she was going to take down a six-hundred-pound copying machine. But with the mood she was in, she knew she could manage it somehow.

"Who's going down?"

Yelping when the voice came from behind her, Sophia jerked upright and smacked her head on the back of an infeed tray. She whirled around to find Reed standing in the doorway, a thick pile of papers in hand. He'd been looking down, most likely at her rear, but he zipped his gaze up guiltily as she glared at him.

She was tempted to snap, *You are for turning me down last night and then ogling me now. Just make up your damn mind and take me or drop me flat already.* But then she reminded herself he had every right to say no to her offer. And he was merely being a normal, red-blooded, heterosexual male for checking out her ass. She had to admit she liked that he found her attractive. But still. It stung that he wasn't so interested in her as a person.

Tears stung her eyes and she lifted her hand to the back of her noggin, thankful it still hurt from smacking into the copying machine's tray. At least she could blame her wet eyes on physical pain.

"This thing," she muttered, motioning to the machine.

"Are you okay?" he asked, coming forward and setting his papers-to-be-copied on a nearby table so he could reach for her. "Let me see." His voice was soft and concerned.

Sophia only wanted to bawl harder because he had to be so freaking nice, a quality that was the exact opposite of every loser she'd dated lately.

"It's nothing," she mumbled, but she let him let him sink his hands into her hair and under her messy bun to feel the back of her head. Lips parting as he smoothed his fingers along her scalp, she lifted her face and looked up at him.

When he reached the tender spot, she sucked in a breath and unconsciously grabbed his wrist.

He winced and met her gaze. "You have a bump."

"Oh." She had nothing else left in her vocabulary to add, so she merely stared into his light grey eyes that looked more silver under these fluorescent lights.

His touch slowed to a stop but he continued to leave his hand buried deep in her hair. Their faces remained inches apart. He licked his lips, and her tummy went all fluttery. She could read his desire loud and clear. He wanted to kiss her.

She wanted it too. Her chin seemed to tilt up on its own accord, aligning their mouths perfectly. All he needed to do was close that small space separating them and seal his lips to hers. When he swayed forward a breath, she swallowed, anticipating his touch, his flavor.

But raised voices in the hall just outside the copying room made him jump back, slipping his hand from under her bun as if he'd been stung.

"Braddock," Marcus boomed at some poor employee. "Where's that file I told you to turn in to Walker this morning? Is he working on it yet?"

As Braddock stuttered a reply, Reed cleared his throat and stepped away from Sophia, transferring his attention to the copying machine. "I take it this thing is acting up again."

"It just ate my report," she muttered, waving the half-sheet she'd managed to save.

He bent down, flipped a switch and in moments had her other half sliding successfully out of the machine. "Here you go."

Sophia's mouth dropped as she stared. "How did you know how to do that?"

He winced. "It's done it to me before."

"Well, someone ought to order a new one. This worthless hunk of junk is going to cost me another hour of makeup work."

"I know. I've already turned in a request to Kendrick."

Something Marcus should've done.

"He had no idea it was so outdated and said a new one should arrive within the month."

Sophia shook her head slowly. "I don't know what this department would ever do without you, Reed. You sure know how to take care of us."

His cheeks flushed. It pleased her that he was so uncomfortable with praise. She would've thought a man with his authority would be more cocky and always seeking the limelight. He was a rare gem indeed, this man she couldn't stop thinking about.

"I still can't believe you don't have a girlfriend," she murmured to herself, not meaning to speak the words aloud. In fact, she hadn't even realized she had until the expression on his face froze.

"Oh God." She slapped her hand over her mouth. "I'm sorry. I didn't mean to—"

He hushed her by grasping her hand and removing it from her mouth. "Maybe I'm waiting," he said.

She frowned. *Huh?* "Waiting for what?"

"Not what. Who." He smiled, a slow spreading of his lips that made the skin around his eyes crinkle with amusement, admiration, and...heat.

As shock arrowed through her abdomen, her eyes doubled in size. Was he trying to say he was waiting for *her*? But hold up. Why would he turn her down if he was actually interested after all? And why wait for her? She was ready now.

Okay, so maybe it really had been a bad time for him, as he'd explained over the phone. She was starting to believe that just might be the case.

Still grinning his sexy, mysterious grin, he dropped his fingers from her hand and picked up his papers from the nearby table before turning for the door and starting out of the room.

"Oh, your copies!" she called after him. He'd forgotten to make his photocopies.

He glanced over his shoulder. "I didn't need any."

Meaning he'd popped in simply because he'd seen her here.

Hope sparked deep in her chest, making her breathing feel tight and stuttered. Maybe he was interested after all. Maybe...maybe she shouldn't give up on him quite yet.

~*~

Danni slowly stirred a pot of stew. She stopped to chop celery, carrots, and potatoes and then plopped them in. Broth splashed out and dribbled droplets across the stovetop. She wiped them away and picked up the large wooden stirring spoon again when Nic came up behind her. He leaned over her shoulder and noisily took a whiff of the steam.

Danni's body tensed, but she refused to move away. He was close enough for her to smell the aftershave off his jaw. His chest brushed her back, literally trapping her between him and the oven with only a little wiggle room to escape.

For some reason, she thought this was a test. If she flinched from him, she failed. If she could remain perfectly still, she passed. But that was silly. Why would Nic care or even notice how she reacted to him? Regardless, she remained motionless while her nerves squirmed and screamed for release.

"That smells good." His voice sent a tremor through her. It was like the rumble of distant thunder that rattled the windows. "What is it?"

Danni concentrated on the pot and focused so intently it blurred. "Vegetable soup."

"Mmm." He made the hum of a satisfied man. As a woman, she responded, and it scared her. Her stirring faltered, but she disguised it by taking the ladle out of the soup and tapping it gently against the rim so clinging liquid would fall back into the kettle.

Nic's arm came around her, just under her arm and between her elbow and waist. She held her breath. But when he started to dip his index finger into the pot, Danni grabbed his wrist.

She sucked in a breath. "It's hot."

Her fingers clamped around him. She could feel his strength as his hand moved despite her restraint. Intent on its purpose, the single digit slid into the stew. Danni's apprehensions peaked, and she released him to escape out to one side, looking up to Nic's face as she did. The stew-dipped finger had just disappeared between his lips.

"It's good," he said. His eyes twinkled with appreciation.

Danni's shoulders almost slumped. She let out a quiet breath. If she had been put to the test there, she thought she'd just passed. She opened a cabinet and pulled out some salt. Nic had moved away from the stove to give her free reign again, and was resting back against the counter with his arms folded as if he were waiting to be the first in line when the food was finished.

She glanced toward Reed, who sat across the room at the computer. He'd paused in his work to glance their way. Danni wondered if he'd felt the tension of Nic making contact with her. But he turned his attention back to the flat screen as if everything was okay now.

Danni sprinkled salt over the soup while Nic studied Reed, his brows knitted into a frown and his stance no longer the lax pose it'd been before.

Something was wrong between them. And in the past few days, it had gotten worse. Only yesterday, Reed had taken Danni to get her cast removed. When they'd returned home, Nic saw her free arm and lit into a big grin.

"Hey," he'd said, coming up and examining the pale skin. "Make a fist." He'd frowned when he gently squeezed the muscles on her upper arm. "We're definitely going to have to whip you back into shape, kid."

During this whole episode, Danni swore Reed had crept protectively closer. But it made no sense. There was no one Reed would trust her with more than Nic.

Something had happened between them when she hadn't been around. And it was causing Nic to glare intently at Reed this very second. Suddenly, Nic pushed off the counter and crossed to the other side of the kitchen, saddling up to a stool and plopping down at the bar, keeping his eyes on his roommate.

"So," he said. "Did you talk to Sophia at work today?"

Danni had tried to appear busy while she eavesdropped, but she kept an eye and both ears on the conversation as she stirred. When Reed's head snapped up, she realized the core of the problem.

Sophia.

Her brows puckered. Who was Sophia? Before she knew it, the question fell from her mouth. Reed spared Nic a quick glare, to which Nic returned heartily, before Reed reluctantly sighed.

"No one," he said. Then he shrugged as if to imply no one important, which told Danni it was the exact opposite. "Just some woman I work with."

She decided the two men must be fighting for this Sophia woman's attentions. But then Nic snorted and whirled on his stool to face her.

"Just some woman?" he repeated incredulously. "Sophia is only just some woman Walker's been talking about nonstop for three years now. I'm telling you, Dan, he's got it bad. I've never seen him so twitterpated before." He laughed and spun back around on the stool to smirk at Reed.

Reed had laser beams for eyes, which he aimed directly at the center of Nic's forehead.

"So did you talk to her?" Nic asked again, his grin wickedly smug.

"Of course we spoke," Reed said, despite the fact his jaw was stiff and unmoving. "We work in the same department."

Nic found a can of mixed nuts sitting on the counter. Sliding them close, he tugged off the lid. "Did she ask you out again?" He popped a handful of peanuts into his mouth.

Out of the corner of her eavesdropping eye, Danni caught Reed sending her a quick glance. Her stomach dropped. Oh, no. This wasn't about Sophia at all.

It was about her.

"No, she did not," Reed said in a voice that was so cold and tight Danni shivered.

He didn't want her to know about Sophia and Sophia's interest in him, while Nic, on the other hand, did want her to know about it. Danni felt caught in the middle.

Some woman wanted to go out with Reed?

Reed wanted to be romantic with a woman?

Her loyalties fell to her brother. But instantly she felt guilty because those loyalties had selfish motives. She wanted Reed here with her in case she got scared. She should have sided with Nic and demanded that Reed pursue the woman whom he'd been talking about for years. But fear clogged her windpipe.

So she changed the subject. "Did they have that accident on the news tonight?"

Both men looked her way. "What accident?"

Danni thought quickly. "Oh, there was a pileup on 429. I guess it was pretty nasty. The noon news said a deer running out onto the roadway caused it." She made herself busy sprinkling more spices into the soup and adding the meat she'd just fried.

Reed glanced at the television. "No, they didn't mention it." He sounded a little confused, no doubt wondering why she was talking about deer.

But she went on as if it were a late-breaking event. "Well, they showed the scene. The poor buck had been slaughtered. You couldn't even tell what it was. I can't believe they actually aired it." She shrugged. "But miraculously, no one else was killed."

She glanced back and caught Nic staring at her hard, as if he'd been betrayed. Instantly, guilt flushed her cheeks. But she refused to let the conversation return to Sophia. She decided to give Nic a consolation prize. More of her trust.

She held out her hand. "Come taste it now."

His eyes fell as he slid off the stool. When his gaze returned, she was holding up the wooden ladle. "Use the spoon this time."

He took the spoon, his fingers brushing hers as he did. When he neared the kettle, she didn't move away, but eased a fraction closer to show her faith. His eyes met hers with a half-smile.

Nic took a few turns around the pot, mixing the meat and vegetables. Danni decided that once she relaxed, he was downright nice to be close to. He smelled good, a pleasant heat radiated off him. She felt a certain excitement, but there was also a security that kept her from becoming alarmed. Actually, she wanted to move closer and soak these feelings into her soul.

Dipping up a spoonful, Nic leaned in to blow out the heat. His forearm bumped her breast, but instead of jumping back, she controlled herself into slowly moving away. When she looked up, his eyes were gleaming. They remained on hers as he sipped from the spoon.

When Danni caught herself staring at his mouth, she sucked in a breath. She watched his throat work as he swallowed. Down her gaze went to an open collar, which she soon became fascinated examining.

When the springs on Reed's computer chair squeaked, sounding more like the crack of gunfire, Danni jerked her eyes up. She gritted her teeth for flinching. Reed had risen from the chair.

"Where're you going?" Nic demanded.

Reed tossed him a glower. "Fire escape."

"Interesting names for those things," Nic said, setting down the spoon. "Since it's where you *escape* to light one."

Reed snapped the window open loudly and crawled outside. Danni winced, glad he hadn't broken the glass. When she looked up at Nic, she noticed the look in his eyes. He was telling her he forfeited.

He touched her arm lightly. "Thanks for the soup."

But Danni knew he wasn't thanking her for the soup. He was thanking her for the consolation prize. Obviously, he accepted her gift of trust in him.

CHAPTER 13

Sophia read the slip of paper in her hand and checked the address. She looked up at the apartment building before her. Well, this was it. Reed lived here. It was an old structure. Brick. But well maintained. The neighborhood was nice. The street was quiet, since it led to a dead end. She rather liked it. It oozed class.

She let out a breath she hadn't realized she'd been holding. She was really here, standing in front of his place. Would he even be home? Sophia kind of hoped not. But then it would only irritate her if she'd gotten all pumped to visit him and he wasn't there. If he was around though, what would he do? Would he be upset because she obviously couldn't leave him alone? Annoyed? Surprised, surely, but he wouldn't actually ask her to leave. Would he?

Sophia bit her lip.

He'd already turned her down once. Kind of. That *kind of* was what had prompted her to come here today. Except he said he needed time. And she wasn't giving him any.

God, she should go. Definitely.

She turned around and was starting back toward her car when she stopped herself. No, she'd come this far. She should at least give him the chance to turn her down again, if that was even what he was going to do.

Movement caught the corner of her eye on the side of the building that had her stopping in her tracks. Reed. He stood on the fire escape on the second floor, leaning against the brick-wall and smoking a cigarette with one knee bent and his foot propped up on the bottom rung of the railing.

Sophia found herself stepping toward him and staring up. He was so handsome in an achy, melancholy sort of way. Never had she seen one man look so lonely. So tormented. She just wanted to go to him and wrap her arms around him.

She cupped her hands around her mouth and was about to call out something funny and entertaining to draw him out of his doldrums, but the curtain of his window parted and a woman stuck her head out.

Sophia's hands fell.

The woman had jet-black hair tied back at the base of her neck. With big, soulful eyes that seemed sad, she crawled through the window. Reed stubbed out his cigarette and stepped forward to hold out a hand and help her onto the fire escape. The woman accepted.

Sophia's heart lurched painfully as the two never let go of their handhold. The woman leaned against him and rested her head on his chest. He kissed her hair and continued to stare down into the empty alley.

Quickly stepping back out of sight, Sophia cowered around the corner and watched Reed and his companion. He'd lied to her. He had looked her straight in the eye and said he didn't have a woman. More than once. But Sophia could clearly see the bond those two shared. She could tell by the intimate, comfortable way they talked to each other, they were close.

Jealousy spiked through her and had her quickly turning away.

Get over it, Eschell, she told herself, and stiffly started marching down the street. *He pushed you away at every turn. Quit acting like you've been betrayed.*

But it hurt. Why had he lied to her? She didn't understand.

She'd thought they were at least friends.

Grr. They *were* friends. They'd had lunch together, and they'd talked, and she'd really liked being with him. It was all very platonic and...and friendly, a lot more friendly than she and Silas Varner had ever been.

Damn it. She wouldn't just tuck her tail between her legs and run away.

Before she could change her mind, she spun back, marched toward the front door and entered the brick building.

The interior was charming. The carpet was a soft mahogany that looked classic. A wide marble staircase led up the center of the atrium. And a small reception desk sat off to the side, where a uniformed man sat sleeping with his feet stacked on the countertop and his arms crossed over his chest.

As Sophia came farther inside, he woke briefly to nod at her, then fell back to sleep. Her gaze was drawn to the staircase. There was an arrowed sign that said an elevator was at the other end of first floor hall, but she wanted to use the stairs. They were enchanting. As she stepped onto the first step, her shoes clicked on the marble and made the sound echo up the stairwell. She took another. Her shoes click-clacked all the way up.

When she got to the second level, the staircase seemed to split, curving up to the third level on each side of the building rather than through the center. Sophia almost wished Reed lived on the top floor so she could follow the charming steps all the way to the top. But she'd already caught his apartment number on one of the doors on the second floor. She slowed to a stop at the crest of the steps and stared.

It was now or never time to chicken out. She chose never.

The closer she drew to his door though, the louder her heart thumped. She stopped directly in front of his apartment and took a deep breath. Then she took another. She raised her hand, knocked, and then quickly dropped her fist as if leaving it suspended for too long would cause some great calamity to happen.

When she heard footsteps, she quickly checked her hair

with her hands, then settled her shoulders back. When the footsteps stopped, she smiled. There was a moment's pause when she knew she was being inspected through the small peephole. Her smile faltered a little during the wait. Maybe he wouldn't even open for her. Maybe it was the roommate looking out…or the black-haired woman.

On the other side of the door, metal jingled from the chain being unlatched. Her heart skipped a beat. As the door slowly opened, Reed's face came into view. She was so relieved and nervous all the air rushed from her lungs like a popped balloon.

"Hi," she said. The breathless word sounded too cheerful even to her ears. It took everything she had to keep from blurting out, *So who's the girl on the fire escape?*

Reed opened the door only wide enough to show his shoulders. She gritted her teeth. The jerk was trying to hide his little girlfriend from view. It figured.

He wore loose-fitting pants and an old t-shirt that seemed to have grown a little snug over the years. Sophia had never seen him out of a suit before. He looked comfortable and downright yummy. Suddenly, she envisioned him like this on a rainy afternoon, snuggled up on a long couch in front of a huge window, matching the pace of the rain outside with his lovemaking.

It shook her, and her smile fell flat so she was only staring at him with wide, crushed brown eyes. Why had he told her he wasn't involved with anyone? Why had he let her hope?

"Sophia?" His voice matched the clothes, a little lazy and a little seductive. He looked around to see if she was alone.

"Hi," she said again. "I was just in the neighborhood." At his confused frown, she continued. "Really. I'm on my way to the Stalanski Bakery. I hadn't realized you lived so close. It's only a few blocks from here, so I decided to stop by and see if you wanted to come along."

Ha! Try to talk your way out of this one, bud.

Before he could refuse, she baited him even further. "They have this really good saffron bread. I can't get enough of it. I'll buy you a loaf so you can try it out because you really have to try it."

Yeah, and then maybe he and his girlfriend could eat it together.

Reed's body remained motionless throughout her spiel. But the expression on his face changed numerous times from shock to pleasure to amusement. It settled on unease. He rubbed the back of his neck and found a spot on the floor between them to inspect.

"Right now?"

Sophia bit the inside of her lip. *Just tell me about her, already*, she wanted to scream.

"I'm kind of settled in for the night." He glanced at his casual attire apologetically.

She was about to say she'd gladly wait for him to change, but she caught movement over his shoulder. Lifting onto her tiptoes, she glanced around him, and there the other woman was. She was almost five inches shorter than Sophia and had big gray eyes that seemed heart-wrenchingly sad. She stared back curiously and a little fearfully.

"Oh, hi," Sophia said loudly, her cheer phonier than ever.

Reed glanced back. When he spotted the woman, he gave Sophia a quick, guilty look that had rage coursing through her veins. Her jaw set, and she knew her eyes had narrowed, but aside from that, she tried to keep her calm. She was about to tell him goodbye and stalk off, when he opened the door wide and motioned with his hand for her to enter.

She blinked. *What?*

"Sophia," he said, looking extremely uncomfortable. "This is my sister."

Sophia stopped dead. She blinked again and then looked back at the woman. His sister?

Oh hell.

She hadn't seen that one coming.

Not even bothering to feel silly about her jealousy, she gave Reed's sister a huge, relieved smile. But thank God she wasn't a girlfriend.

Okay, maybe she'd jumped to conclusions a little too

quickly. But after looking from Reed to the black-haired woman, she paused. Hmm. Something was still strange about the situation. Reed glanced toward the young woman he'd just labeled his sister, giving her an apologetic wince. Sophia followed his gaze.

"Danielle?" she said. She didn't know why she said it so softly, as if talking to a scared five-year-old. When she crossed the threshold, the girl took a step back. Her face was pale as she huddled against the kitchen counters.

"It...It's nice to meet you." Danni's voice was quiet and shy. She ducked her head.

Sophia could only gape. *This* was the great children's author she loved? It didn't seem to fit. The Danielle Walker stories she'd read were full of life and fun, exciting tales. The woman before her seemed almost ghostlike. All she needed was a completely white sheet to finish the look.

She still didn't know why, but she continued to address Danni with that adult-to-child voice. "I love your stories. I bought one for my niece last Christmas."

Danni nodded. "Thank you."

"You look totally different in life than you look on the back cover of your books. I didn't recognize you."

Instead of responding, Danni looked to Reed for support, and Sophia found herself doing the same thing.

He stuck his hands in his pockets and stood awkwardly between them. "Uh..." He took a moment to glance at Sophia with eyes that pleaded for understanding. That only confused her more.

"Danni's been visiting us for the past few months."

"Oh." Sophia frowned, trying to find the true meaning behind his words. She looked to his sister, whom she now realized looked a lot like Reed. "Where are you from?"

Danni looked frantically at Reed and then back. "Here in town."

Sophia opened her mouth to respond nicely, but then snapped it shut. If she was from here, then why did she have to stay at Reed's?

But Reed quickly input, "Danni usually stays at her college dorm, but...she's taking some time off for...for her writing, so..." He shrugged.

Sophia stared at him. He was a terrible liar. His answer was so obviously not the truth she almost told him so, but after a glance at Danni, who'd somehow gone paler, she decided to let it slide.

"So...she's been bunking here," Reed finished, making his lie stand out even more baldly.

Sophia nodded. The door stood open at her back; she had the urge to duck out and dash away, but movement farther inside the apartment caught her attention. She braced herself for more discomfort as all three of them glanced at the man who entered the living room.

A bit shorter and slimmer than Reed, he wore his hair lighter and longer. His shaggy head remained bent as he read a magazine. In a t-shirt and jeans with a hole in the knee, he scratched his chest through the shirt and strolled toward them, intent on reading his article.

"And this is my roommate, Nic," Reed said, causing the man to stop and glance up.

Bright blue eyes that were startling with their intensity glanced between Reed and Danni before they zeroed in on her.

"This is Sophia," Reed told the roommate before she could speak.

Sophia felt a smug satisfaction when the roommate's jaw dropped in recognition. Obviously, he'd heard about her. It had to have been good reports too to get that kind of response.

Nic's attention swerved to Reed before a mischievous grin lit his face.

Then he swept forward past Danni and stuck his hand out. "Dominic Calhoun," he introduced pleasantly, wiping the unease from the air as if he'd just sprayed a can full of awkward-be-gone into the room. She shook his hand and smiled. His grip was firm but light. She liked him instantly.

"But call me Nic." Then he tugged her a fraction of an inch closer and spoke almost into her ear. "Or anytime." He said it loud enough for his roommate to hear. Then he risked a glance toward Reed, who glared back.

Sophia laughed. She definitely liked the roommate. "I'm Sophia."

Nic smiled, his eyes playful. He had yet to let go of her hand. "Sophia...?"

"Oh! Sorry. It's Sophia Eschell."

"Eschell?" he said, wrinkling his nose. "No, that won't do at all."

Sophia jerked her hand away from him. "I beg your pardon?" How dare he make fun of her name? She loved her name.

"Just bear with me a second," he said, and easily slipped an arm around her shoulder. Then he spread his hand out before them as if reading a billboard. "Now imagine this. Nic and Sophia Calhoun." Then he glanced over at her and wiggled his brows. "What do you think? Sounds better, doesn't it?"

She rolled her eyes. Oh, this flirt was definitely trouble. She couldn't believe she'd ever thought he was gay, though in her defense, she hadn't known him at the time.

Reed quickly came to her rescue, thumping Nic on the back of the head with the palm of his hand. Nic let go of Sophia and turned to Reed defensively.

"What? She can tell me to piss off if she wants."

Reed pointed a stern finger at him. "Behave."

"I am." Nic efficiently ignored Reed by turning back to her. "Come in for a drink, Sophia." He took her hand again and glanced meaningfully at Reed as he pulled her into the kitchen. "Get the door," he instructed.

Reed shot him a scowl but shut the door. They passed Danni, who gave Sophia a timid smile, the most cheer Sophia had seen out of her since they'd met.

"We've got tea, soda, beer, wine, water, milk..."

Sophia laughed again, overwhelmed as he rattled out a dozen more choices. When he was finished, he looked at her as if to say, *Well, what'll it be?* Her smile faded when she glanced at Reed. He looked absolutely miserable. He'd come up beside the scared-looking Danni and stood stiffly, looking completely out of his element.

Hating the turmoil she was obviously putting him through, Sophia smiled tightly at Nic. "Actually, I'm going somewhere. I was just…" What had she been doing? Making a total fool out of herself. Again. "Dropping by on my way through to say hello."

Nic's face fell. "Really? That's too bad." He shot a quick, disappointed look Reed's way, pinning the blame on him. "We were just getting ready to play some cards." He strolled over to Reed and set a hand on his shoulder. "And Walker here needs a partner."

Reed gave Nic a steaming look.

"Oh, I, uhh…" Sophia had no idea what was going on. But she knew Reed didn't want her around.

She was trying to come up with a graceful way to decline when Danni spoke up. Sophia sensed it surprised not only her, but both men as well.

"I hope you're not that good at Pitch. I've never played before." She sent Nic a hesitant smile and then looked toward Sophia again. "But Nic and Reed are pros. It would even out the teams better if we had another amateur playing."

Nic's mouth had fallen open. He shut it and then let it fall once more. "You've never played Pitch?" He turned to Sophia, clutching his heart. "See, you've got to stay now. Have mercy on this poor girl, or rather on me, since I'm doomed to be her partner." He came up behind Danni and set both hands on her shoulders.

Sophia swore Danni sagged away from him, but then she seemed to stop herself. She looked up at him and smiled, bolstering herself. "Please stay," she said to Sophia.

Then Reed finally spoke. "The Stalanski Bakery doesn't close until midnight as I recall. There would be time for you to go there afterward."

Sophia's gaze shot to him. He continued to look worried and a bit ill, but there was also a hopeful expression in his eyes, and that's all she needed to see.

"I suppose I could fill in for whoever's missing."

"That a girl!" Nic whooped and came around to take her arm. "Now about that drink. I've got a great Concord chilling. You like red wine, right?"

He led her toward the kitchen, leaving the brother and sister behind.

"Oh, nothing alcoholic, please. I'm driving." She risked a glance back toward Reed, but he was too busy staring oddly at his sister to notice.

CHAPTER 14

Reed touched Danni's arm as Nic charmed Sophia in the kitchen. The worried glint on her face as she looked up made his stomach muscles tighten with his own worry. "Are you sure this is okay with you?"

Though her eyes were large with fear, Danni nodded. "It's perfectly fine." She took his hand and squeezed.

He squeezed back and almost said, "Thank you," but was able to stop himself in time. Glancing toward his roommate, he watched Nic smooth his way into Sophia's good graces. He was making her laugh again as he opened cabinet doors and rummaged through the contents for a drink. Inside were only canned food products.

"Hmm. Let's see." Nic pulled down a short, fat can. "I suppose you could have some tuna juice if you wanted."

Sophia chuckled and glanced toward Reed. He rolled his eyes and returned the grin.

"I think I'll pass," she answered, keeping Reed's gaze.

"Sure?" Nic said, looking from her to the can.

She wrinkled her nose. "Positive."

"Oh well." He stuffed the tuna back and shut the door. "I guess that concludes our options of beverages to choose from.

So what'll you have?"

Suddenly, Reed was glad Nic was there. He could get caught up in his friend's cheer and good humor and forget about Danni's problems for a while.

"Let me see." Sophia tapped on her chin with a long nail, and Reed instantly went hard. What the hell was it about her damn, sexy nails that always made him want sex?

He swallowed and spun away, feeling guilty for thinking about all that in front of his sister.

"I'm going to hunt up some cards," he mumbled, and took off toward his bedroom just as Sophia said she'd take iced tea.

"Iced tea? Is that all?" Nic sounded put out at the simple request. Then he shrugged. "One iced tea coming up."

In his room, Reed took deep breaths and waited for his woody to subside. When he exited his room, toting a deck of cards, he found Sophia moving closer to Danni.

"Is he always like this?" she asked of Nic.

For an answer, Danni nodded. The two women suddenly grinned at each other.

Nic was reaching up into a cabinet for some cups, and Danni darted in behind him. She touched his arm, and he looked down. When he saw it was her, he jerked back, startled.

"I'll fix the drinks," she said, taking the cup out of his frozen hand. "You guys go set up the table."

As if in a hypnotic trance, Nic followed her orders. "Okay." Then he smiled at her fully. "Sure."

Everyone was seated by the time she carried the drinks over on a tray. She sat a cupful before each person. Sophia looked up and smiled, saying thank you. Danni took her seat. Though she was on Nic's team, she sat across from Reed.

He figured his matchmaking roommate had arranged it that way so he could be beside Sophia.

Nic dealt and Reed immediately picked up his cards and checked his hand. Danni followed suit, but Sophia looked around.

"Wait a second. Aren't you going to explain the rules?"

Reed exchanged a chagrined glance with Nic, and they spent another ten minutes going over the rules. Sophia asked questions while Danni sat quietly and listened. They played a couple of rounds with their cards facing up, to get a feel for the game, and then they started in with the real match.

Nic and Danni won the first round. Nic leaned over to nudge Danni's arm. "You're a natural," he told her.

Danni smiled lightly.

Reed almost rolled his eyes at the lying pair. He and his sister used to dominate Nic and whoever he'd gotten to partner him whenever she used to come visit them in college. And she might be good, but he was better. So he and Sophia won the next round. When Sophia started to catch on, Danni pretended to do better too. And finally, the game grew intense.

At first, Nic asked Sophia questions about herself or Sophia would talk to Danni about her writing. Reed remained quiet unless spoken to, but he listened to everything around him, soaking in the conversation, the thrill in Sophia's laughter, the glow in her beautiful brown eyes. He wanted to consume her whole.

He felt high on adrenaline. The three most important people in his life were suddenly gathered around one tiny table. It was so surreal but wonderful, thrilling yet cozy. He didn't want the game to end.

But before he knew it, they'd reached the last round. Each team was close enough to go over the top score so that whoever won this hand, won the game. Nic looked up at Danni halfway through the play. She nodded. His shoulders relaxed a little, but then Reed set down a high card and snagged a few points for him and Sophia. But Danni surprised them all when she sat down a ten and took the rest of the points.

"Yes!" Nic jumped from his chair, victorious. "Oh my God, Danni, you're amazing." He grabbed her and pulled her from her chair, giving her a smacking kiss on the lips as he tightly hugged her.

Obviously unprepared for his enthusiasm, she screamed and

wrenched away.

Nic instantly let her go. But as she stumbled, off balance from his sudden lack of support, he once again caught her arm before she toppled over her chair.

Reed surged to his feet.

"Danni! I'm sorry," Nic gushed immediately, making sure she was steady on her feet before he stepped away to give her space.

Reed moved in, but she held up her hand, and he stopped, giving her space too. "No, I'm sorry. I overreacted." As the two men hovered anxiously and protectively on either side of her, she covered her mouth with shaky hands. "I'm so sorry."

She looked across the table at Sophia, the only person still in her seat, and burst into tears. Sophia stared from Reed to Danni to Nic in astonishment, looking as if she wanted to bolt for the exit.

Irrationally irritated with his roommate, Reed slugged Nic in the arm. "What the hell, man?"

Nic raised his hands defensively. "I'm sorry. I forgot." He fell dejectedly into his chair and stared at his feet. "I forgot."

"Why don't you think about what you're doing next time? Jesus Christ!"

"Dude," Nic shot back. "I'd have done the same thing to *you* if you'd been my partner. I was celebrating the win."

The two guys glared each other down.

Danni grasped Reed's arm. "It's okay," she tried to soothe, even as she trembled from head to toe. "I know Nic didn't mean any harm. It's my fault."

"It's *not* your fault," Reed objected. "Stop apologizing. I hate it when you apologize. *You did nothing wrong!*"

He caught Danni glancing toward Sophia, and after his own glance, he spun away from them all to run his hand through his hair. "Damn it."

Sophia must've taken that as a sign. She surged to her feet. "I should get going. Thank you, everyone, for the drink and lovely evening. I...I'll see you later."

Nic didn't bother to stop her, and Danni could only sniffle

out a sob.

Reed turned toward her. "No," he said, and reached for her arm. But then he dropped his hand and closed his eyes, whispering a curse. He didn't know what to say to explain any of this.

"I think I showed up at the wrong time," Sophia said quietly, her gaze apologizing. She glanced to Nic and Danni and then settled on Reed. "I didn't mean to barge in."

Reed couldn't meet her sad gaze.

"Good night," she said.

He nodded, his heart tightening painfully in his chest. No. *No!* He didn't want her to go.

Suddenly, Danni grasped his arm. "Tell her, Reed."

Sophia paused and looked back.

Reed forgot to breathe as he stared at his sister. When he was able to shut his mouth, he shook his head. "Are...are you sure?"

Tears clogged her lashes as she nodded.

Tugging her into a bone-crushing hug, he could feel wetness soak through his shirt. "Thank you," he whispered in her ear.

When they pulled away, each sibling wiped their eyes with the back of their hands. Reed looked at Sophia, who appeared stunned speechless.

He blinked a few times. "Would you like to take a walk with me?"

She nodded. "Yes. Yes, very much."

He started toward her, but paused and looked back to Danni. Nic had gotten to his feet.

"I'll be back," he said, sending a brief glance toward Nic.

Danni backed up next to Nic to show she had no fear of him now. "Okay."

Nic looped his arm over her shoulder. "We'll be fine," he assured.

Reed nodded and ushered Sophia to the exit.

~*~

113

"Want to see if we can make it to the bakery before they close?" Reed asked, closing his apartment door behind them.

Sophia glanced over and took in the solemn look on his face. Feeling impatient and wanting to demand what the hell was going on, she bit down the urge and managed to coolly answer, "Not really. Let's just...walk."

"Okay." He nodded and led her to the elevator. They were the only two inside when the doors closed. Reed was quiet and Sophia decided to follow his example. But being alone with him in such an enclosed space caused her body to heat. She wanted press her mouth against his and—

"Danni was raped," Reed said quietly.

Sophia spun to him, her jaw dropping wide. "*What?*"

Reed wasn't looking at her. Instead, he studied the lighted numbers above the door. When the elevator stopped, he stepped out and started walking. Sophia hurried after him.

He didn't speak again until they were out of the building and marching along the sidewalk in the cool night air.

"The Friday afternoon I left early from work," he said. "That's when I got the call. She was alone in her dorm room in the middle of the afternoon. She'd just taken a shower and was in her bathroom when someone knocked on her door."

Eyes widening, Sophia cupped her hands over her mouth. "Oh, Reed. No."

"When she first checked her peep hole, no one was there, so...she took the chain off in order to see further into the hall." Pausing in his story, Reed quickly dug into his pocket until he pulled out a squashed package of cigarettes. His hands weren't steady as he tugged one free from the rest.

Sophia suddenly reached out and caught his fingers, keeping him from lighting up. "Don't," she said.

He lifted his face. They stared at each other for a good ten seconds. Sophia soaked up all the agony she could see in his face, and her eyes filled with tears.

"God, this is awful, Reed." She blinked rapidly.

Reed lifted his eyes toward the sky. "Please don't cry," he

said in a choked voice.

"I can't help it. It's just so horrible. Poor Danni. She's so sweet. So…" Unable to take it any longer, she stepped toward Reed and hugged him.

His muscles tensed at first. But she merely snuggled closer, pressing her cheek against his shoulder. He relaxed a second later and even lifted his arms to wrap them around her in return. And wow, did it feel good. Sophia clutched him tight and let herself sob.

"Stop it," Reed said in a tight voice. The shudder that followed told her he'd begun to cry, too. He buried a hand in her hair and rested his face alongside her neck.

"I'm so sorry," she whispered.

"It's not your fault." He lifted his head and look away as if embarrassed for crying all over her, but his body stayed molded against to hers and his fingers remained in her hair.

The light from a streetlamp above them caught a tear on his cheek like a prism, and it sparkled against his skin. She reached up with her index finger and caught the droplet. When it clung to her skin, Reed turned his head toward her.

"Neither is it your fault," she said.

Then she lifted up on her toes and touched her mouth to his. A small whimpering moan of need came from the back of his throat. His soft lips moved against hers, seeking more. The hand in her hair slid down until his thumb grazed the side of her throat. The light touch of his mouth teased. Sophia found herself pressing closer.

He let her, following her lead and taking her tongue into his mouth as soon as she sought entrance. Then he returned the favor, stroking the roof of her mouth. Sophia's knees went weak with desire. She grabbed two handfuls of his coat and clung to him, unable to separate her lips from his.

Anxious for more, her fingers flattened over his chest and she moved her hands down, pausing at his waist, where she tugged at the hem of his shirt to pet his perfect abs. He sucked in a breath and pulled back slightly, detaching their lips.

He looked down at her fingers at his waist, breathing hard.

She grinned. "Too fast?"

He stared a moment before his lips lifted. "Too public."

Sophia blinked and glanced around to find them standing in the middle of a sidewalk. She blushed. "Oops."

Reed chuckled and leaned his forehead against hers. She basked in the sound. This was good. He was relaxed and laughing.

Kissing his neck, she said, "Want to go someplace private?"

"Yes," he answered immediately, catching the corner of her mouth and nibbling. "But I need to get back. Nic freaks when he's stuck alone with Danni for too long. He's not…he's not too comfortable about being around her yet. Not since…"

Sophia nodded. "I understand."

Reed stared at her a moment. Then he lifted his hands to cup her face. She didn't think he was going to touch her for a second, and then he did with the barest of pressure, the pads of his fingertips hardly grazing her cheeks. The wonder in his gaze told her he couldn't believe she was letting him do this. She closed her eyes and tipped her head back, sighing deeply.

"Someday," he said in an aching voice as he pressed his forehead to hers. "When Danni is better, I want to continue this."

Sophia opened her eyes and smiled. "Are you asking me out, Reed Walker?"

His eyes glittered with fervor. "I don't know when I'll be able. It'll be a while before she can—"

Sophia stopped him by pressing her lips to his for a soft, yet full kiss. It successfully shut him up. "I'll wait," she said as he stared at her mouth, obviously wanting more of it.

He nodded. "Thank you."

Feeling revived and happy, Sophia took his hand. "I guess we should get back then."

She started to turn back toward his apartment building but he yanked her into another hug. "I changed my mind."

Sophia lifted her face. "About what?"

"Friday. I want to see you again on Friday. And I don't mean at work."

CHAPTER 15

When Reed made it home, he found Nic and Danni on the couch. Asleep, Danni rested her head on Nic's chest as Nic looped his arm around her shoulder. The television ran with the sound turned low. As Reed door shut behind him, Danni opened her eyes and raised her head.

She blinked and brought Reed into focus with a tired smile. Slowly, she pushed to her feet and rubbed her hands up and down her arms. Nic stood as well.

"Is everything better?" Danni asked.

Reed stuck his hands in his pockets and nodded.

"Sophia's nice," she said.

"Yeah," he agreed.

"And pretty."

He nodded again, sheepishly.

"You should ask her out." Danni went to him and hugged him. "I'm happy for you," she murmured. He thought he might start tearing up again, but she stepped back before the urge intensified. "I think I'll turn in for the day."

He touched her hair. "Good night."

Danni looked to Nic, and he lifted a hand. "Sleep tight,

kid."

As she slipped into Reed's bedroom and softly closed the door behind her, Reed fell onto a stool at the kitchen bar and sighed heavily. Nic came over and leaned his arms on the counter across from him.

"I told you Danni would be okay with it."

"Thank God," Reed said, and scrubbed and hand through his hair. "Because I already asked Sophia out."

Nic laughed. Reed threw him a look to shut him up, but his roommate ignored it. "So where're you taking her?"

On a bed, was Reed fist instinctive answer. But he knew that's not what Nic meant. He stared at the top of the counter. "I, ah, we haven't gotten quite that far on the plans yet."

Nic laughed again. "God, Walker. You're a sorry sight." Then he leaned closer and murmured, "Hey, if you forgot how it goes, I'll be glad to give you a few pointers."

Reed only glared before he shook his head and chuckled. "Shut up." But his smile didn't last long. His worry showed through the lines on his brow. "But I do need a favor from you."

Nic caught onto the seriousness and immediately nodded. "Just name it, man."

"You seemed okay with Danni when I came in," he said, instead of asking a question. "You seem better about everything."

Nic nodded. "Yeah, I am better. A lot better."

Reed stared at him a moment. Then he said, "Do you think you could stick around here while I'm gone?" He glanced toward his bedroom door and Nic's gaze followed his. "I haven't left her alone at night yet. I'm sure she'll be okay. But I'd feel better if…"

Nic nodded slowly. "I think Danni will do just fine. But, yeah, I'll stick around." He snorted. "It's not like I have any plans anyway. Not with the way my social life has gone lately." He sighed, then stretched. "A night in will do me good."

"Thanks."

~*~

In her kitchen, Sophia tasted her family's mystery sauce. She bit her lip and added a few more spices before tasting it again, hoping the flavor wasn't too strong. The timer for her bread went off, and she tossed the spoon aside, snagged a pair of oven mitts and opened the oven door. The bread better be a perfect golden brown or she was throwing it away. Nothing could be burned. Nothing could be tasteless or have too much garlic. Nothing could be short of perfect. Amazing and unbelievable as it was, Reed would be here any minute.

She opened the oven, wincing even before she could see the results. Then she pulled the pan out and expelled a relieved breath. "Thank God." She shut the oven door with her hip and brought the golden brown bread to the counter to flip it over onto a waiting cloth.

The table was already set for two. She checked the clock; it was about time to light the candles, though once she did, she worried they might scream seduction. Did it look too romantic? She deliberated whether she should turn on a few more lights and flipped on one more in the dining room.

Of course, a seduction scene was what she was going for, but she didn't want it to be too obvious. She wanted to look like a tidy little homemaker. In a frenzy, she straightened the magazines on the coffee table in the living room, then fluffed pillows on the couch. She'd just started back toward the kitchen when the doorbell sounded.

Sophia froze. Oh Lord, was she ready for this? Had she been too forward, inviting him to her home on their first date? Gah, was she going to just stand there, petrified, and make him wait forever?

Smacking a hand to her forehead, she raced to the entrance. When she noticed she had no shoes on, she groaned. Would that look too informal? It was probably more of a clue into her seduction attempt than the lighting. She made a sound of distress and hunted up a pair of slip-ons that matched her outfit. She was belly crawling under the couch and almost had her hand wrapped around the last shoe when the doorbell gonged again.

She jumped and whacked her head against the bottom of the couch. Sitting up dizzily and putting her shoe on with one hand while trying to pat her hair back into place with the other, she called that she'd be right there. Things were going great so far, she thought bitterly. She staggered to the door and waited a second so she could regain her equilibrium. Then she dabbed at the sore spot on the back of her head to see if it was bleeding. When her fingers came away clean, she opened the door.

He had on a tie and a casual sports jacket. Wearing a pair of Dockers, he looked polished and a little nervous. His eyes quickly skimmed up her blue jeans and collared shirt. But when they settled on her face, she forgot all about nerves, the fresh bump on the back of her head, or even their mismatched attires. Their gazes locked, gray to brown.

"Hi," he said.

She grinned foolishly before she realized she'd been keeping him out in the hall. "Hello. Do come in, Mr. Walker."

She stood aside, letting him in. When she closed the door at his back, he stepped from the front hall into the living room and studied her living space. Sophia came up beside him and looked around as if seeing it for the first time as well.

She had a flowered futon in the center with a cherry wood coffee table in front of it. Dozens of framed pictures sat on top of a trio of shelves that hung from the wall. They were all of her family.

Reed started to remove his jacket and Sophia worried if she'd set the heat too high.

"Here, I'll take that."

He handed it to her, and she hung it from a coat rack by the front door, trying not to breathe in his scent wafting off the cloth. Then she paused and stood a moment, staring at their jackets hanging from the same tree. When she turned back, he was once again studying her living room with a curious eye.

"The kitchen is this way," she murmured, feeling shy all of the sudden.

She spun on her heel and started through the dining area.

Her skin tingled in excitement when she heard him follow. As they passed the opened door of her bedroom, she glanced inside to make sure she hadn't left a stream of clothes piled on the floor or anything.

She almost stumbled to a stop when she saw she *had* forgotten to make the bed. Oh dear, if that didn't look like a cozy invitation, she didn't know what would.

She risked a quick glance back at Reed and noticed that's exactly where his gaze had landed. Well, she hadn't been shy thus far about pursuing him. Why start now, huh?

"I hope you brought an appetite." She winced, hoping that hadn't sounded like some kind of sexual overture. "Because I've made us plenty of food," she finished lamely.

Reed's attention seemed reluctant to leave the bedroom doorway, but then it traveled toward the cupboards and stove in the kitchen section. "It smells wonderful."

She told him to take a seat while she served the meal.

But he shook his head. "I'll help."

She nudged him into a chair. "No. You're the guest."

He sat and watched her bring over a basket full of bread with the steam still rising from them. And then she brought a large bowl of salad and finally the main course: Spaghetti with meatballs.

Reed grinned at her. "Are you going to sit down now?"

"Maybe." She slid into the seat across from him. They stared at each other across the candles.

"Sophia, this looks amazing," he said. "But really, you didn't have to go to so much trouble just for me."

She smiled and then laughed. "Lord, do we sound formal or what?"

He flushed in return. "I guess we do."

She fixed her gaze on the tabletop as well. She hadn't thought up a dinner conversation. "Oh, I forgot the wine."

She was already half out of her seat again when he commanded, "Sit."

She gave him a startled look.

He rolled his eyes. "I'll get it. In the refrigerator, right?"

She could only nod. When he rose, she slid back into her chair. She checked the table while he was gone to make sure nothing else was missing. Reed called back asking where the corkscrew was kept, and she gave him directions as she found a napkin and settled it under a dripping candle.

When he returned, he'd taken off his tie. "You didn't have to lose the tie." She'd daydreamed way too many times about taking one off him.

Reed patted his neck where he'd undone the top button. "I wanted to." He poured their wine and then sat down.

And their evening began.

Sophia eased him into conversation. Mainly she asked questions about Danni. As he drank, he talked about his sister with more ease. And as he talked about the better times, Sophia could see the sadness drain from him. She realized this was a healing process and urged him to continue. Soon, she was only listening while he spilled story after story. She could tell by the animation on his face that the best times of his life had been his college years when he'd first met Nic, especially the times the two of them had snuck Danni into their dorm room and spent the night watching action movies.

Somewhere in there, they ate until they were full.

After they finished their meal, Sophia carried the dishes to the kitchen sink and stored the food. The last of the wine was only a sip left in each of their glasses. She urged Reed to go into the living room and wait on her as she cleaned up.

He agreed, and by the time she joined him, he lay passed out on her couch. Sitting at one end of her futon with his head lolled back, Reed looked deep in dreamland.

Disappointed, Sophia's smile died, though okay, she did like the way his eyelashes rested against his beautiful cheekbones. But that still didn't mean she wanted to bore the man to sleep on their first date.

With a sigh, she settled on the opposite end of the futon and tucked her bare feet up under her. Resting her chin on her knees, she watched him.

She was tempted to reach out her toe and nudge him back

to consciousness, maybe ask if she was really that dull. But he must be bushed, so she let him be. He looked really comfortable, and warm, and stimulating. She wondered what would happen if she crawled over next to him and cuddled against him. Maybe she could wake him in some very inventive way.

Deciding to do just that, she started his way. He didn't even stir, which caught her sympathies and made her stop.

"Oh, Reed," she cooed softly. "You poor thing; you're exhausted." She lightly touched his cheek. It felt wrong to disturb him now.

She crawled off the futon and searched up a stray blanket and pillow.

When she returned to him, she took off his shoes and set them on the floor. Then she settled his stockinged feet on the opposite end of the small couch. After draping the blanket over him, she leaned over his head and wiggled a pillow under his cheek.

Their faces were so close when she did; she gave in to temptation and kissed him lightly on the mouth.

He made an unintelligible sound and turned his face her way as she backed off.

"Smells like Sophia," he mumbled. His hand came up and reached in her direction, but his fingers fell blindly as he drifted back into unconsciousness.

Sophia picked up his warm, limp hand and squeezed. Her heart pounded down into her knees as she fell in love with the man fast sleep on her couch.

CHAPTER 16

Screaming woke Nic from a deep sleep. Jarred alert, he jerked straight up in bed and gasped. Heart leaping into his throat as the blood-curdling shrieks continued, he nearly pissed his pants.

The hair on the back of his neck stood at attention as he blinked through the pitch black room, seeing absolutely nothing in the dark.

The noise sounded like it was coming from right under his bed. It vibrated through his mattress and shook him to the bone. He put a hand down to brace himself. If he lived in California, he'd have thought it was an earthquake. But then he realized the sound came from behind the wall.

He panted, out a breath. "Oh no. *Danni*!"

His roommate would murder if him he let anything happen to his sister on the one night Nic was supposed to be responsible for her.

Scrambling off the mattress, he got tangled in the sheets and fell to the floor with a thud. Cursing, he banged his knee. He managed to stumble to his feet and race from the room, only to smack into the closed door of Reed's room.

"Danni!" He grabbed his nose with one hand and reached

for the doorknob with the other. But it was locked. He pounded on the door with open alarm. "Danni, are you okay?"

He searched the wall for the light switch and flipped it on. He pounded and yelled again. But it was unlikely she could hear him over her own screaming. The chilling noise made his breathing accelerate. It sent the fear racing straight through his bloodstream. He squared his shoulder and charged the door. Wood splintered and he gained entrance.

The light from the living room spilled onto the bed. The solitary figure that thrashed against blankets covered her own throat with an arm and squeezed her eyes shut as she continued to open her lungs.

Nic stood a moment, almost too frightened to approach, but then he flew inside. He took her frail shoulders in his hands. "Danni?" He shook her lightly. "Danni, honey. Wake up."

When she shied away from him in her sleep, he shook harder. "*Danni*," he shouted.

Finally, her eyes sprang open. At first, she tried to escape. But he only pulled her closer. "It's okay. Everything's fine. You just had a nightmare."

He repeated the quiet words until she stopped struggling. "Dominic?"

"Yeah. It's me." He smoothed the hair from her face and made her focus on him. Tears streamed down her cheeks. "Are you better now?"

She shook her head. "No. No, I'll never be better again."

A sob claimed her, and Nic pulled her to him for an encompassing hug. She clung tightly. "It's okay, Danni. Everything's okay. You're safe."

But she only cried harder. Her body trembled; she began to hyperventilate. Nic had no idea what do, so he held on tight and rocked her. "Shh. Danni, don't."

Maybe he should call Reed's cell and get his ass back home. But Walker needed a night out. He needed a good dose of Sophia. So Nic held Danni closer and told himself he could deal with this. Not that he believed himself.

"I thought…" She tried to talk, but it was hard through the tears and the stuttered breathing. "I thought that day was the darkest hour of my life. But I was wrong. I was wrong." She sobbed and whispered. "This is." She pounded her fists against his chest. "Make it go away. Make it stop."

Nic's arms tightened around her. "Oh God, Danni." His voice broke. "I can't…" What should he do? Helpless, he clung to her, his chin wobbling from his own rising emotions. "Danni, stop." His arms tightened, and her fists fell limply at her sides, making him worried he'd just suffocated her.

But she continued to shake. "I don't want to do this anymore," she sobbed. "I don't want to hurt Reed. I don't want to hurt you. I don't want…I don't want…"

"You've got to quit fighting yourself," he said, suddenly soft. He rubbed a hand over her head and pressed her face into his neck. "Talk to me."

She shook her head. "No."

"Yes," he said, suddenly steady. "Let it out, Danni. Don't hold this in anymore."

"I can't." Her hands fisted in his shirt. "I don't want you to know."

"The hell with that." He grabbed her shoulders and pulled her back. Her eyes widened when she saw his blazing gaze. Tears glistened on her cheeks. "Tell me," he demanded. "Tell me now."

Danni's face fell. "He raped me," she whispered.

The breath shuddered out of Nic, and he winced. Suddenly, he didn't want her to talk. He didn't want to know. He pulled her to him and cradled her in his arms, wishing she wouldn't say anymore and realizing that Reed had been right. He shouldn't have pushed because he couldn't listen to this.

But she kept going. "Except in this dream…it wasn't the last guy. I…I dreamt about the first rape. I dreamt *he* was hurting me."

At first, Nic was sure he'd misheard her. But when he repeated her last words in his head, there was no way he'd been mistaken. Going still, he forgot to breathe as he whispered, "What? What first rape?"

"When I was little," Danni said. Her fingers clutched his shirt into desperate fists as she buried her face against his neck, making each syllable echo through his throat as she spoke. It burned his esophagus as he swallowed.

"I don't...I'm not sure how old I was. I was little. Reed was in middle school, I think. It...It was one of my mother's ex-boyfriends."

Middle school age? If Walker had been twelve or thirteen, then Danni only would've been five or six.

"Oh, my God," he managed to utter. Oh, Lord. No. "You were raped when you were *five*?"

"No." She shook her head violently. "Not me. But I saw it. I watched it happen. I remember it."

Nic's head went a little light, all dizzy and disoriented. "Who? Your mother." No wonder Walker had always been so freaking protective of her. She'd been forced to watch her mother get brutalized when she was only—

But Danni whispered, "No. Not Joan."

Nic frowned slightly. "Then who—"

"Reed..." Danni paused to lick her lips. She lifted her face from his chest; her big grey eyes bore into him as she hoarsely answered, "Reed was raped."

CHAPTER 17

Reed jerked awake on a gasp. Sweat coated his face. He had no idea what had roused him. He'd been having a deep and dreamless sleep, something that had been very elusive lately. Then suddenly, he was wide awake.

Instantly panicking, he began to gasp for breath.

He lay in pitch black, instinctively knowing he wasn't home. As he coached his breathing back to normal, he realized he lay stretched on some kind of couch. He was well acquainted with the stiff-necked, muscle-cramping sensation that sleeping on a couch wrought.

Man, he missed sleeping in a bed.

Groaning and rubbing at the back of his neck, he sat up and threw his feet over the side to set them on the floor. Where in the world was he?

And then it struck him. Sophia. He'd been on a date with the woman of his dreams. The last thing he remembered was waiting for her on her futon and closing his eyes as he sank into her too-soft cushions and drowned in blissful oblivion.

Pausing, he sniffed the air and smelled her earthy fragrance. He was still in her apartment. He'd gone and fallen asleep on her flowered futon.

Feeling like a complete ass, he patted the floor around his feet, hoping to find his shoes. It was purely by luck that his fingers stumbled across them.

He couldn't believe he'd fallen asleep on her.

She must not have been too upset about it, however, since she'd taken his shoes off and thrown a blanket over him. God, she'd even put a pillow under his head.

Disappointment rose; he'd been looking forward to tonight all week long. Actually, he'd been looking forward to this for three years.

How could he do this to her?

Cautiously stretching to his full height, he decided he could really do with a light right about now. Wow, it was dark. He hated the dark. Bad memories came in the dark.

Suddenly claustrophobic, he spread his arms out to feel for a wall, or hopefully some kind of light source. His breathing grew choppier.

He swung around, arms outstretched, trying not to panic when his hands plowed into the side of something. Reed skidded to a halt, but it was already too late. Things toppled over and crashed to the floor. At the sound of glass breaking, he let out a string of curses.

"Reed?" Sophia's voice called from down the hall.

He closed his eyes, though he wasn't sure why. He couldn't see anyway. He brought a hand to his face, feeling awful. Whatever he'd broken had completely shattered.

When he opened his eyes, a light came on down the hall. Footsteps approached. Glancing down, he finally saw what he'd wrecked. Biting back another list of obscenities, he immediately crouched in front of the mess. He'd taken out a whole shelf of pictures. Glass had been busted out of every frame.

The living room light blinked on, nearly blinding him.

"Reed?" Sophia called in a concerned voice.

"Watch out," he cautioned sharply, throwing out his hand over the glassy mess.

Sophia stopped.

"They're broken." He picked up the largest pieces and piled them together. "I'm sorry. I didn't mean to—"

"Don't worry about it." Sophia crouched beside him and started to help. "I should've left a light on for you. But you were so out of it I honestly thought you'd sleep through the entire night."

"I'm sorry about that too," he said. "I can't believe I fell asleep on you."

"Reed," she said softly. Patiently. "Don't worry about it."

"No," he argued. "It's not okay. I—" He lifted his head to give her a proper apology, eye to eye, but as soon as he saw what she was wearing, the words froze in his throat.

She was in some kind of silky red top with nothing but spaghetti strings keeping it from slithering off her shoulders and showing him how she was not wearing a bra. And, oh dear Lord, one strap was already threatening to fall. Then there were her shorts. They were made of the same silky red fabric and were so blessedly short, showing off the long expanse of legs that had driven him crazy for three excruciating years.

He stared, unable to take his eyes off her body for a good ten seconds. Then his gaze slid to hers. "You're..." he managed to get out. But that was it.

"I was sleeping."

He nodded dumbly and his eyes fell again. Her unconfined breasts swelled against the silk and when her nipples hardened through the cloth, he sucked in a harsh breath.

Oh, God, he was losing it.

Springing to his feet, Reed stood and tore his eyes away, forcing himself to stare at the wall. "I should go," he said in a high voice.

Sophia slowly rose to her feet as well. She was quiet a moment before murmuring, "Or you could stay."

His gaze jerked to her. When he saw the longing in her face, a zap of electric current rippled through his body, almost taking him to his knees.

He nodded and was a little breathless when he answered, "Okay."

Sophia sent him a slow smile that slipped inside him and settled hard in his gut. Then she held out her hand. "Let's go to my room."

Entranced, he took her warm fingers and let her turn toward the door. But when he stepped forward, broken glass crunched under his shoe.

"Shit, I forgot." He immediately started to bend and return to his cleaning duty, but Sophia tightened her hold.

"Later," she said and tugged him back up, forcing him to follow her.

He did. All the way to her bedroom. She reached for the switch to turn off the light, but he caught her hand.

"I want to see you," he said as he moved his fingers up her arm until they hooked the frail strap. Making sure his knuckles grazed the tops of her shoulders as he did so, he lowered the red string, watching the v neckline dip as he slowly pulled it off until her top pooled down around her waist, caught a second on the swell of her hips and then fluttered the rest of the way to the floor.

He couldn't believe this was happening. Why was she letting him touch her? Why couldn't she tell she was way too good for him?

Instead of questioning her, he took what she offered. Kissing his way across the tops of her shoulders, he purposely kept himself from touching or even eyeing her fully exposed breasts.

He trailed his fingers up and down the smooth expanse of her back and reveled in the satiny feel of her skin. God, she felt so good. She shivered when his tongue came out and tasted the flesh on the side of her throat.

"Reed," she murmured, threading her fingers through his hair before she tugged at his shirt. Soft hands and long nails came around his waist and he shivered. The sensation of her nails on him was so strong that it shot out the ends of his toes. He groaned and pulled her closer.

Wanting to go slow and easy, he backed her toward the bed, putting a few more inches between them so he could tug off her shorts. Sophia opened his pants, working his zipper.

Stripping her of her last remaining bit of clothes, he removed her panties and dropped them to the floor. Sophia stepped up to him and coaxed his head down, sucking his tongue into her mouth. Her naked body pressed against his. He could feel every blessed warm inch of her. Her soft, heated skin was heaven.

But he was going to explode too soon if he didn't watch it.

Pulling back to see her fully, he cupped her breasts, his palms delighting in the weight. Then he swiped his thumbs over her nipples. She gasped and arched. Bending, he licked the tip of one rosy bud.

"Reed!" Sophia grappled for him, and ended up yanking handfuls of his hair.

He sucked the nipple and entire areola into his mouth. Her breathless pants were music to his ears.

"Don't stop, don't stop," she chanted.

Scraping her breast erotically with his teeth as his tongue toyed with the peak, he curved his hand around her hip and settled her back on the mattress, climbing over her so he could fit himself into position between her thighs. He touched her bent knees on either side of him, awestruck that they were actually there.

"Now," she commanded, arching her neck back so her long strawberry blond hair flowed like silk over the mattress in a move that woman had sensuously perfected throughout time to bring a man to his knees.

Drugged under her spell, Reed obeyed. After protecting them, he pressed his hard, ready length against her swollen, moist folds. He paused to enjoy the view, to savor the moment. Back bowed with her breast pressed into his hands and her eyes fluttered closed in sweet anticipation, Sophia Eschell was the most beautiful specimen he'd ever witnessed.

He wanted to tell her he'd waited his entire life for this very moment. To be permitted into something so special and perfect was humbling. His stomach tightened and his breath held as he slowly pressed forward, unreasonably fearing he'd be denied entrance.

But her slick body accepted him. With a gasp, he rocked deeper. His vision wavered and dimmed. Oh, God, he was going to pass out from the ecstasy of it. He groaned and closed his eyes, too consumed to think.

Once he was fully embedded and buried as far as he could go, he paused and parted his lashes to once again take in the sight of being united with Sophia's.

"Dear Lord," he rasped.

She grinned up at him, her eyes heavy-lidded and slumberous. Stretching out her arm, she cupped his cheek, caressed the growing bristles on his jaw, then stroked down the side of his neck and over his smooth chest. "Go ahead, gorgeous man," she murmured. "Rock my world."

His body throbbing for release, he pulled free and thrust back in. She cried out and lifted her hips to meet him.

Forcing the tempo to steady and slow so he didn't hurt her, so he wouldn't fly off the handle and split her apart by how hard he wanted to pound, Reed clenched his jaw.

He hoped she didn't feel him shake. But their union was so powerful, it unsettled him. She made the most enticing sounds, panting and gasping, moaning at the just the right time. Pressure built at the base of his manhood, tightening his muscles, coiling and building.

He continued to watch her face, relishing the way her eyes went unfocused as he stretched her.

"Faster," she encouraged, digging her nails into his back. "Oh, God, Reed. It's coming. I can feel—"

She cried out, writhing and consumed.

He lost his focus and pounded without finesse. As her inner muscles clamped around him and pulsed, he snapped. The tightly bound pressure he'd balled up inside him exploded.

He squeezed his eyes shut and groaned as all the energy inside him bolted forth, releasing a fury of emotion and lust. Her thighs clutched him hard until the last wave of passion passed.

Spent, he collapsed on top of her, completely boneless.

He could've sworn he passed out, because when conscious thought returned, his breathing had slowed to normal, and so had Sophia's. She lay quietly under him, stroking his back and resting her face against his neck.

"Sorry," he slurred and fumbled to roll off her. "Am I crushing you?"

Sophia clamped her legs around him, keeping him in place. "No! Don't go. I like you here."

He settled but shifted some to the side so he was half on the mattress. "Thank you," he murmured.

She chuckled. "Why? You were all warm on top of me, like my very own Reed blanket."

"No." He frowned. "Not for that. For...for everything." Lifting up so he could see her face, he touched her cheek just to make sure she was real. "Thank you for tonight. You make sex beautiful."

Her smile was a little watery. "So do you," she whispered, leaning up to kiss him.

~*~

"So where was I?" Sophia asked. She sat cross-legged in the center of her bed with Reed curled around her in a nest of tangled sheets.

"Gary," Reed reminded her as he opened his mouth expectantly.

Digging a spoonful of Chunky Monkey from the tub on her lap, Sophia held the ice cream out to him. He dipped his head before closing his mouth around the treat. As she pulled the silverware free, his eyes lifted to hers. Something powerful dropped into the pit of her stomach.

She wanted to own this man. She wanted every little piece of him all to herself. She wanted to know him inside and out.

"What was Gary's fatal flaw?" he asked, his eyelashes heavy with lack of sleep. His gaze settled on her face even as he smoothed his hand up her bare thigh and leaned forward a couple inches to kiss her knee.

Sophia swallowed. Even dead tired, he could manage to look drop-dead sexy. "He was married," she reported.

Reed's eyes opened wider, suddenly very awake. "You dated a married man?"

She rolled her eyes and took her own bite of ice cream, delighting in the cold, wet flavor against her tongue. "Not knowingly. Geez. What kind of girl do you think I am?"

"A very sexy, sensual, sweet, sensitive one," he answered with a dreamy smile while his palm curved around her hip.

Shivering with awareness, Sophia stroked his thick hair. "And a stupid one, too. Obviously. I can't believe I didn't know he was married. I'm only thankful I didn't sleep with him before I found out."

"So am I." Reed kissed a couple inches above her knee this time.

She fed him another spoonful of ice cream. As a dribble of chocolate caught at the corner of his mouth and began to leak down his chin, she leaned forward and licked it away. He caught her before she could retreat. Kissing her, he drew her closer and slid his tongue into her mouth, tangling it with hers.

She moaned and sank against him. The cold tub in her lap did nothing to cool the heat stirring inside her.

Reed slowed the kissing to occasional pecks until he spoke against her mouth. "So this would probably be a bad time to tell you I'm married, huh?"

Sophia froze until she felt him smiling against her mouth. Slugging him in the arm, she muttered, "Jerk," only to kiss him again.

He laughed.

As he moved his mouth to her throat and then her shoulder, she scooped out the last of the Chunky Monkey. Offering it to Reed first, she swallowed the last bite after he shook his head.

"So who's next?" he asked, seemingly fixated with kissing and nibbling his way down to her elbow.

She sighed, thinking he could continue with this kind of treatment forever. "Next," she repeated the word, thinking hard. Who'd been after Gary? No one except—

"Oh, that brings us back around to Silas."

"The drunk," he confirmed.

"Right. He called me last month and said he was in town. Wanted to stop by and see me. Said he'd stopped drinking."

"But he hadn't," Reed guessed.

"No, he had. Si's as clean a whistle and happily married. He just wanted to swing his new, gorgeous wife by and flaunt her in my face."

"I doubt she was prettier than you," Reed said as he caught a particularly sensitive part on the inside of her arm.

She gasped and closed her eyes, reveling in the sensation.

"Next?" he prompted.

She shook her head. "No next. That's it. That's the entire sordid history of Sophia Eschell's love life."

"Doesn't sound so sordid to me."

"No, it sounds sad." She turned to him, making him lie back among the blankets and pillows so she could set her empty ice cream tub on the nightstand and crawl over him to dot his chest with kisses. "But from here on out," she continued between pecks, "I'm turning over a new leaf. No more liars. No men with baggage. No deep, dark secrets or haunted pasts. Just normal, average, everyday guys."

Reed slid his fingers through her hair without responding.

Once she kissed her way up to his mouth, she settled beside him and snuggled close. With a sigh, she rested her head on his shoulder. She couldn't remember feeling this peaceful and satisfied in a long time.

"Will you stay the rest of the night?"

Reed was quiet. Alarmed, she lifted up to see his face.

He looked like he was in pain. Instantly worried, she touched his cheek. "Reed? What's wrong?"

He shook his head and rolled his eyes. Immediately his expression cleared. In an amused voice, he said, "Let me think about this. I can either stay here in a real bed with a sexy dream come true or I can go home to a couch that's too short for me. Gee, what *ever* should I do?" He wrapped an arm around her waist and nuzzled his face against the back of her neck. His legs moved against hers in a sweet caress. "I would be honored to stay the rest of the night with you."

Sophia couldn't quite believe it. The man was a cuddler. She loved that.

Smiling, she ran her nails over the side of his ribcage. "Oh, so that's why you're staying, huh? You're using me for my bed."

"Yeah," he murmured lovingly, pulling her closer so that he could kiss her hair. "*That's* the only reason I'm here."

Sophia sighed. She couldn't help it. She was just so happy. She reached out to turn off her bedside lamp. But he surprised her when he caught her wrist and gently pulled her hand back.

"I want to watch you fall asleep," he said, making her let out another contented little sigh of delight.

As she retracted her hand, a strange, passing thought struck her. This wasn't the first time he'd prevented her from turning off that light.

A frown marred her brow as she began to drift off. Was Reed Walker afraid of the dark?

~*~

Nic was pacing the kitchen like a caged animal when a rested and relaxed Reed slipped in the front door. Even before the latch clicked shut, Nic attacked.

"Hi," he said in a breathless voice as he turned and pinned Reed with an anxious look.

Reed paused, surprised. He hadn't expected Nic to be awake so early. He usually slept in on Saturday mornings, sometimes staying in bed in until nearly noon.

Wishing Nic wasn't seeing him looking as he did, Reed scowled. His shirt was rumpled and untucked, his hair could use a comb, and he was coming home from his date at seven in the morning.

Bracing for the ribbing to begin, Reed was beyond surprised when Nic scanned him with concern. He looked restless, worried. It caused Reed's stomach to knot instantly.

"What happened?" he asked immediately.

Looking immensely guilty, as if he'd just been caught doing something naughty, Nic's eyes flashed to Reed's face. "Nothing," he said. Then his lashes dropped as if he could no longer hold the stare.

"You're acting weird," Reed said, eyeing his friend warily. "And you're awake. What's going on?"

Nic sighed and rubbed his face. "Danni had a nightmare last night."

Reed's body became still and his face drained of color. He immediately started for his bedroom, but Nic spoke.

"She's in the shower." He lifted his hand in reassurance. "And she's fine."

"Why didn't you call?"

"Uh-huh. That would have worked out real well." He tucked a hand to his ear and mimicked a telephone. "Hey, Walker. Could you put your pants back on and get over here. Your sister's screaming bloody murder." He dropped his hand listlessly. "Yeah, that would've solved everything."

Suddenly, Reed's hands fisted. "I told you, Calhoun. I told you she wasn't ready. And look what happened."

Nic gave him a frown. "Oh, like it wouldn't have happened if you were here?"

Reed shrugged. "Maybe. How could we know?"

"Because, Danni needed to—"

"Oh, here we go again. You still think you know what she *needs*."

"As a matter of fact—"

The door to the bathroom opened then, shutting both men up. They looked toward Danni with guilty eyes.

"Good morning," Nic said, stepping toward her. "How do you feel?"

"Better," Danni answered. She glanced from man to man. "Are you guys fighting?"

"No," they answered in unison.

Danni's lips twitched with amusement. "Could've fooled

me."

Nic took another step toward her, but stopped. "You need more sleep."

Reed gave him a sharp, suspicious look, wondering where this sudden protective attitude was coming from.

Danni shrugged. "Why?" She smiled again and looked around the room with bright eyes. "I feel...rested." Her gaze settled on Reed. His dropped. "Good morning, brother."

"Morning," he mumbled.

She glided to him and kissed his cheek. "Coming in at seven." She chuckled as she pulled away. "You better tell me you had a good time last night."

Shamefaced, he lifted his groggy gaze but said nothing; could only give a brief nod. Danni smiled again and hugged him. Reed closed his eyes and hugged her back. "Good," she said and backed away. "Now, if you'll excuse me, gentlemen. I need to dry my hair."

She sent a smile toward Nic, who nodded and tucked his hands inside his pockets. Then, grinning, Danni spun away and practically skipped into Reed's bedroom. Reed watched her go, astonished. He'd never seen her so happy—not since the attack, anyway.

He rounded on Nic. "What the hell happened last night?"

Nic merely shrugged. "I told you. She had a nightmare."

"And *that's* why she's so chipper this morning?"

Nic studied him a moment. "Look, Walker." His voice was kind. "Don't worry about Danni so much. I'm here too, you know. I'll help out. Don't think you have to handle everything on your own. I took care of things last night."

Reed looked down at his hands. His chin quivered. "I should've been here."

"Well, you weren't. And look how well that turned out. Have you seen her smile like that since the...the...well, you know?"

Reed looked up, irrationally pissed he hadn't been able to make her smile like that. "Since when did you become her white knight?"

Nic sighed. "Since last night," he retorted. He shook his head and glanced away again.

Something didn't seem right with his roommate, but Reed couldn't quite put his finger on what was wrong.

"You don't have to do this alone anymore," Nic assured him, acting too nice for his normal self. "I'm here. And I want to help."

Reed stared hard before Nic fidgeted and glanced away again. Shaking his head, Reed murmured, "Whatever." He marched toward the window and pulled it open, before climbing out and searching up his cigarettes.

CHAPTER 18

Birthdays brought about celebration on the accounting floor of Kendrick Advertising. Since the department had no official courtesy committee, Sophia and a handful of other women ensured every accountant whose birthday they discovered was thrown a party in recognition.

She and another woman named Gretchen took care of supplying the treats, while Brittney sent out the email announcements, and Myrna printed out a birthday card for everyone to sign. During their 2:30 break, every accountant on the floor crowded into the break room for a bit of tension release.

Today, the birthday honor fell to Winston, a sixty-three-year-old, pencil-thin man whose thick mustache was bushier than the stray sprouts growing on top of his head.

With her back to the entrance of the break room, Sophia was busy beating the pants off a forty-year-old grey-headed accountant named Davis at a throwing game they'd devised a year earlier when a hot shiver of awareness passed up her spine. She instinctively knew Reed had arrived.

A split second later, Myrna said, "Reed?" in a surprised voice. "Uh…can I help you with something?"

Finishing her toss and hitting the exact cup to make her win her match, Sophia ignored the cheers and glanced over at the same moment Reed shifted his gaze to her. Time stopped. Pinned under the silver magnetism of his gaze, she forgot to draw oxygen into her lungs as she watched him stare back.

She hadn't seen him or even talked to him since the morning he kissed her goodbye at her front door. Looking at him now, decked out in his professional suit and tie, she could barely recognize the man who'd become her lover only a few days ago. It was as exciting as it was intimidating to face him now, surrounded by coworkers—exciting because that polished, unattainable-looking man was all hers, and intimidating because…well, for the same reason.

Someone cleared his throat, or shuffled, or something, because it shook Reed back to reality. He jerked his gaze from her to return his attention to Myrna.

"Never mind," he answered, his voice low and humble, though it still managed to send a thrill through Sophia. Filled with images of their date, she continued to watch him as he glanced down at his shoe and murmured, "I didn't realize you were on your break. It can wait."

Then he turned on his heel and started back toward the exit.

"Hey," Sophia called after him before she could stop herself. Around her, her coworkers stiffened and glanced at her in surprise and silent warning.

Slowing to a halt, Reed stopped for a moment with his back to her before he leisurely shifted around, his eyebrow arched in question.

"You didn't eat a cupcake," she accused with a reprimanding grin full of teasing as she lifted one of the treats from the counter, where it had sat next to the coffer maker. She held it out toward him.

He glanced at the pastry in her hand, looking tempted and causing another kind of temptation to stir deep in her own belly. Then he lifted his clear grey eyes and opened his mouth as if he were going to apologize.

She frowned, no idea why he looked so regretful.

But instead of explaining himself, he glanced around them at everyone who'd gone deathly quiet at her cupcake offer.

"No, thank you," he declined formally before pivoting away, his entire bearing almost angry as he marched from the break room with rigid precision.

Like flipping a switch, the tension in the air lifted, and everyone immediately loosened, returning to their idle chatter. Scowling, Sophia stared at the spot where he had stood. Ignoring the next accountant challenging her to a throw-off, she mumbled, "Excuse me," and hurried after Reed.

As soon as she sprang into the hall, she turned in the direction that led to his office and saw the back of his jacket as he strode away.

"Reed," she said loud enough for him to hear.

His shoulders stiffened as he halted, but when he turned to look at her, his facial features still looked more regretful than angry. She hurried to reach him.

"What's the deal?" she asked, utterly confused. They were alone in the large open area comprised of cubicles; almost everyone was still crammed into the break room, having fun.

Reed gave his own confused frown. "What do you mean?"

She set her hand on her hip. "How could you turn down one of my cupcakes? I just made them this morning."

"You did, huh?" he asked, his eyes warming as he sent her a grin that reminded her once again of everything they'd shared together. A hot flush blanketed her as he reached out and carefully slipped the treat from her suddenly limp hand. "In that case," he murmured, his eyes settling her way as he licked a sample of frosting off the top. "I would be honored to nibble on this."

He turned as if to leave her standing there, gaping after him.

"Wait a second," she grumbled. How dare he turn her on and then just abandon her like that.

Pausing yet again, Reed glanced back. "Hmm?"

She pointed back toward the break room. "Don't you want to eat it with the rest of us?"

His gaze lost some of its sparkle as he stole a brief, shadowed look over her shoulder. Then he shook his head. "No."

Totally baffled, she demanded, "Why not? You never come to any of the birthday parties we throw, and I don't understand it. I know you don't think you're too good for us."

For a moment, he merely studied her. Then he quietly cleared his throat and glanced down before mumbling, "I wasn't invited."

Sure she'd misheard him, Sophia leaned closer. "You weren't *what?*" When he lifted his eyes, she knew she'd heard him right. Her mouth dropped open. "No, that can't be right. Everyone's invited, Reed. Well, except...Marcus."

His tight smile told her how wrong she was.

"But that's...How could...Brittney's in charge of sending out the emails. She must've just forgotten."

He winced. "I don't think she forgot."

With a sniff, Sophia scowled at him. "Of course she forgot. Everyone on this floor thinks you're a god. No way would she deliberately..." But her voice trailed off as she continued to watch his face.

"I'm never invited, Sophia."

Shaking her head to continue denying, Sophia blinked, hoping if she fluttered her lashes enough she'd see him smile instead of sending her a weary look.

"But..."

"It's fine," he assured her. "I know I don't...fit in."

Rage, swift and violent, rose in her throat. The injustice of it made her fist her hands at her sides.

She couldn't believe this. How had she never noticed how much her coworkers had ostracized him? Sure, his weight with Kendrick was a little intimidating. He poised himself as a figure that demanded respect, but she'd never thought of him as someone to be cold-shouldered before.

"I cannot *believe* this," she fumed. Without warning, she snagged his forearm, gripping him through his polestar sleeve. Dragging him along behind her, she marched with a clenched jaw back toward the break room.

"Uh...Sophia." His voice was uncertain behind her even as he followed without resisting. "What're you doing?"

"I'm taking you to the break room," she growled. "You're an amazing man, and it's about time everyone else figured that out."

He stopped walking, jarring her to a halt. When she spun back to scowl at him, the soft, achy look in his eyes caught her off guard.

"Sophia," he whispered, lifting his hand as if he wanted to touch her face. But an inch before making contact, he dropped his fingers and sighed, closing his eyes. "You don't know how much your thoughtfulness means to me. But don't force me on them. You'll only make everyone uncomfortable."

Studying the creases of sorrow in his face, Sophia decided she'd rather have everyone else uncomfortable than make this man experience one more second of exclusion.

"I'm sorry, but I don't care about them." Her resolve was set. "Come on." Marching back into the break room, she didn't give him a chance to escape as she strode through the doorway and lifted her voice, "I challenge Reed Walker to a throw off."

"To a what?" he said behind her just as all conversation stalled and every eye turned their way.

Keeping her grasp on him so he couldn't escape, she grinned at him. "A throw off," she explained. "It's a game we play at every birthday party."

"I don't..." He began to shake his head, but paused as he glanced around, making Sophia realize the two of them had captured every eye in the room. Clearing his throat, he offered her a tense, tight smile. "Okay. What're the rules?"

She beamed, happier than she could express that he was actually going to play along. "It's easy. We set up a Styrofoam cup in the center of the table and take turns trying to throw a paperclip into it. Best four out of seven wins."

Scratching his chin idly as he studied the single cup sitting in the center of the small break room table, Reed asked, "What do we win?"

Sophia shrugged. "Anything we want. Each player sets the terms before the game."

Eyeing her thoughtfully, his voice dropped an octave as he asked, "So what're *your* terms?"

Her belly quivered and the first answer to pop into her head was a kiss. She wanted a kiss from him right now so bad. But she cleared her throat, ignored the heat rising up her neck, and drummed her fingers over her lips as she thought. "Hmm."

She looked down at her outfit: skinny jeans, a long tight light-blue sweater that rode down to the bottom of her thighs and cinched at her waist with a black and diamond-studded belt. Setting her hand on the belt, she lifted her face with an ornery grin.

"If I win, you have to wear my belt for the rest of the day."

The room grew oddly quiet. She could actually feel everyone hold their breath as she issued her challenge, as if they felt she'd be fired or something for saying such an outrageous thing to *the* Reed Walker.

Reed studied her before asking, "And if you lose?"

She sniffed. "Not going to happen. But go ahead." She waved a hand. "Name your own terms."

Just as she had, he skimmed his apparel before grasping his tie and smoothing his long, tapered fingers down the length. "Fine. You have to wear my tie for the rest of the day."

Finally, people around them began to relax. A few even chuckled at Reed's return terms of the game.

Sophia shrugged as if she didn't care one way or another, though the idea of wearing a piece of Reed's clothing thrilled her a heck of a lot more than it mortified.

"Have it your way. But you are so going down, Walker." Turning her back to him, she took aim, focusing on the Styrofoam cup. "I think the sparkles in my belt are really going to bring out the grey in your eyes."

"Just throw," he said, his voice dry, yet amused.

Grinning, she did, and missed her target. With a gasp, she whirled to send him an accusing glare. Just as she suspected, his eyes glittered with suppressed glee. Around them, everyone whooped, booing her on.

"Hmm. Too bad," Reed murmured, nudging her aside so he could take his turn.

"Best four out of seven," she reminded on a growl.

When he sank his first paperclip into the cup, two men standing close to Sophia laughed and nudged her, needling on her defeat.

She held up her hands, quieting them. "Hey, he hasn't won yet."

What followed were two of the most intense minutes of her life. She and Reed managed to draw the game out for as long as possible, making every onlooker hang on their every word and movement. It was thrilling, being the center of attention with him. They harmonized so well together, even their audience seemed to fall into an excited, anticipatory mood.

It was impossible to concentrate, and not just because people continued to call things to her as she took aim. With the man who'd stayed the entire night at her house only forty-eight hours before standing at her elbow, close enough she could smell his aftershave and feel his body heat soaking into her left arm, she could barely focus on the cup, much less throw straight. She missed her second throw as well.

When Reed made his fourth shot in a row, the game came to an end. She'd only made two of her first four tosses; she'd lost. With a shout of triumph, the victor pounded his hands into the air and spun toward her to beam out his success. Even his teeth seem to gleam with life and excitement. His subordinates cheered him on, making his lips spread even wider.

Sophia had never been so tickled to lose a match in her life. Meeting his grin with an arch of her eyebrow, she murmured, "*Touché*."

"Tie, tie, tie," the accountants around them chorused. "Make her wear the tie."

Grey eyes still glittering with joy, Reed's gaze stuck to her as he slowly lifted his hand to his throat and loosened his tie.

Swallowing, she watched, unable to take her eyes off him, mesmerized by how handsome he looked, easing the slim strip of cloth over his head and widening the noose before lifting it again to grin at her. Why were men so freaking hot when they undressed?

"Ready?" he asked, his voice so low and sexy she shivered.

Trying not to seem too eager, Sophia lowered her head in submission. He slipped the noose past her hair, briefly catching it on one of her ears. After tugging it free with his finger, he settled the tie in place around her neck, and gently gathered her hair free of any constraints. Instead of leaving the tie hanging loose around her neck or even letting her tighten it into place, he kept a handhold on the knot and used it as a leash to urge her a step closer to him.

He looked at her so intently she knew, just *knew* he wanted to kiss her. Her belly tightened and her face even lifted to receive the warm press of his mouth. But instead of following through with the promise in his eyes, he smiled a full, beautiful smile that took her breath.

"I hope you're not a sore loser."

After finding it difficult to talk, she swallowed. When had her throat gone so dry? Unable to take her stare off him, she managed a swift shake of her head.

"Good." He tightened the knot, not enough to cut off air, but just snug enough to claim ownership. She gulped, feeling heat from the cloth where it had just lain against its previous owner.

She very nearly sighed. He was so never getting this tie back.

If there weren't so many eyes watching them, she would've yanked him against her and kissed the shit out of him. She would've wrapped her arms and legs around him and never let go.

His grey eyes glittered as if he could read every naughty thought in her head. "I need to get back to work," he said, making her blink in shock. "Thanks for the cupcake." In his expression, he thanked her for more than just a cupcake.

She opened her mouth, but no words came out.

With one last smile, he swung away and swept from the room. Sophia watched him go, feeling forever changed.

"Sweet mercy," Brittney trilled, catching Sophia's arm and laughing out a girlish giggle. "That was, by far, the sexiest thing I have ever seen. I had no idea Reed Walker would look so good without a tie…" Then she winked. "Or with one."

Sophia blushed and glanced around to find everyone talking about what they had just watched, each similarly surprised by how human and personable the legendary Reed Walker really was in person. Though she was pleased she'd gotten everyone else to accept him readily into their clutches, she was also disappointed. It had been kind of exciting hiding Reed's affability all to herself. And now that they'd become an item, she wasn't so sure if she really wanted to share him with the rest of the world.

He was supposed to be hers. But now that she'd ousted his true nature, what would keep someone like, oh say Brittney, from pursuing him? Feeling suddenly sick, she wondered if she'd just doomed herself.

~*~

Later that afternoon, Sophia was still cursing herself. In the basement of Kendrick, she rummaged through the old storage room for an unused cabinet to organize her mounting records. She sighed and glanced over her shoulder before opening another drawer to an ancient, creaking metal drawer. The old fluorescents flickering overhead cast wavering shadows around her, making her arms prickle with unease.

The walls were made of a crumbling water-stained concrete and exposed pipes ran across the low ceiling. She could hear the people on the floor above walking around. Sometimes, if someone particularly heavy passed, dust would scatter off the pipes and fog the already dim room.

She shivered and thought she might have heard footsteps in the hallway. But when she glanced at the doorway to the storage room, no one appeared.

No one would bother coming down here, anyway, unless it was the janitor. She turned back to her task. Hurrying her pace, she yanked open another drawer to see if the next cabinet was empty, thinking the faster she got out of here, the better.

Suddenly, the single light in the room went out. She froze, her heart jumping sporadically in her chest. Stupid basement wiring. When the door behind her clicked shut, she yelped.

Oh God. Someone was in the room with her.

The first word that popped into her head was rape. Danni's miserable, chalky face floated through her head.

Her breathing escalated.

It was black, so black she could only see splotches of light from where the long bulbs had been glowing overhead. She tried to remain calm and quiet, but failed miserably. Air shuddered from her lungs loudly. If she could manage to be quiet, maybe he wouldn't find her. But her heart sounded like a banging drum, leading the attacker straight to her.

"Sophia?" a voice said, and she almost screamed. He had to be only five feet away. "Where are you?"

When sanity caught up with her, she frowned. "Who—"

"It's me," he said, sounding more familiar. And closer.

"Reed?" she gasped.

Long, familiar fingers found her arm. She grabbed him and pulled him close for a bone-crushing hug before she slugged him in the chest.

"What're you doing," she hissed. "You scared the shit out of me." Then she heaved him back to her for another reassuring hug.

"Sorry," he whispered. His fingers combed apologetically through her hair. "I didn't mean to scare you. I just wanted to…I want to overcome a fear."

Sophia wrinkled her brow. "A fear? Of what? The dark?" She let out a snort at the idea of the mighty Reed Walker being afraid of the dark, until she remembered wondering that very thing at her apartment.

When he didn't contradict her, she swallowed down a rush

of uncertainly. This just didn't seem possible. Reed was an intimidating, powerful, confidant figure in the company. Hell, people were so cowed by him, they were even too afraid to invite him to the office birthday parties.

She opened her mouth to ask him about it, but he kissed her silent, sucking her suspicions right from her mind. His lips were hot and wet and urgent. She cupped his head, and his tongue scraped over her teeth, tickling the roof of her mouth. She felt the caress all the way out the ends of her toes, where they curled inside her heels.

"When I'm with you, I feel like I can overcome anything," he murmured, trailing his lips along her jaw and nuzzling his nose just under her ear. His hands rode low on her hips until they smoothed around over the swell of her ass.

"Y-you *can* overcome anything." She gasped when teeth nipped her lobe. "You're Reed Walker. Everyone looks up to you. You're Kendrick's golden boy."

He huffed out an amused sound as if he didn't agree with her. "Yeah, and I couldn't even get an invitation to a simple birthday party until you came along."

She couldn't believe her ears. The man she'd fallen for had always seemed so confident, self–possessed. He didn't act as if he needed anyone or anything. Everyone else relied on him and he easily supported any accountant who came to him for help. This new side of him stumped her. She'd had no idea that inside him dwelled a man with any kind of fear or insecurity, a man that needed someone else to lean against.

Just when she thought she was getting to know the real Reed, he confused her and threw another layer onto his personality. Realizing whatever troubled him had to run deeper than his latest heartache with Danni, Sophia wanted to know him even more. She wanted to climb inside his head and discover every little secret this quiet, complicated fellow contained.

But she didn't particularly want him to know she was growing so obsessed. Determined to lighten the mood, she leaned against him and nipped playfully at his chin. "You know,

I'm really starting to regret introducing my coworkers to this personable side of you. Pretty soon, women are going to be flocking to you, and you'll forget all about little ol' me."

His laugh was quiet, yet husky and amused, while his nose trailed into her hair and he inhaled her scent. "I highly doubt that."

Arching her neck back to allow him access to lavish her throat with more loving pecks, she continued to argue. "Deny it all you want, but Brittney's already half in love with you."

"Then I'll just tell Brittney I'm already half in love with someone else."

A jolt slammed through Sophia, catching her breath. She froze in his arms, wondering if he was serious or simply teasing. The mere idea of him being half in love with her sent her whirling.

He didn't seem to notice what he'd said either, because he continued to hold her and nuzzle, sprinkling kisses over her face. Tempted to admit she was more than half in love with him right back, she even opened her mouth to confess all, but fear kept the words lodged in her voice box.

Playtime coming to an end, Reed kissed her one last time before pulling away. "I need to get back to the office."

"No," Sophia whined, winding her arms snugly around his neck. "Just one more kiss."

He complied, palming her buttocks as he pulled her flush against him. Sophia could smell his minty breath on her face before he kissed her once more. His lips were hot and wet and urgent. She cupped his head, and his tongue scraped over her teeth, tickling the roof of her mouth. She felt the caress all the down between her legs, and she suddenly wished she wasn't in a skirt so that she could wrap her thighs around his waist. Reed jerked her blouse out of her waistband and his fingers found bare flesh. They both moaned.

"I need to feel you," he said abruptly.

His fingers fled her waist and were suddenly at the backs of her knees. They caught the hem of her skirt and slid up her thighs so that the cloth came up to her waist. He backed her against something solid. It must have been a table or desk of some kind because she was suddenly propped up on top of it and Reed had managed to wedge his hips between her thighs. Their bodies pressed intimately together. The only thing stopping him from being inside of her was their underwear. She didn't know when he'd unzipped his pants, but they'd already been pushed down to his knees.

Sophia bound her legs around him and slipped her long nails into the back of his underwear to cup his buttocks and pull him even more snugly into the cleft of her heat.

He gasped and said something that neither of them could understand. Kissing her ardently, he grasped her panties and peeled them down her legs.

"I don't have anything," he whispered suddenly, as if just remembering that.

She squeezed her eyes closed. "I'm on the pill. Have been for years to regulate my…"

Oh, Lord they were going to make love, right here in the basement of Kendrick. She'd never felt so excited from this kind of risk before. The table was cold and bare under her bottom. But when it mixed with the shaft of thick heat that entered her, her body turned to liquid. She was so wet that he slid straight to the hilt. They both sucked in a breath. She could hear his teeth gnashing.

"Sweet Christ," he muttered. "I've wanted to be inside you since I put that tie on you earlier."

As if just remembering she was still wearing it, he gripped it as he kissed her hard, holding the cloth around her neck to anchor her to him. "Putting this thing on you so was goddamn sexy, I wanted to take you in the break room."

"Diddo." She nodded and kissed him back, desperately.

When he started to move, he shuddered and wrapped his arms around her so snugly that their breastbones touched. The darkness was heavy around them, it made her feel out of breath. Or maybe that was Reed making her breathless. In any event, she panted for more oxygen.

At the back of her mind, she wondered if it was really Reed

moving inside her. She couldn't see his face and hadn't seen his face since he'd come into the room. He could be anyone really.

But she knew his voice. She knew his smell, and she knew the feel of her lover sliding in and out of her.

She came so quickly and powerfully that she bit his shoulder, getting a mouthful of his shirt. She tasted the cloth and squeezed her eyes shut, trying not to scream. She pulled him inside her 'til she swore he touched her heart.

He made a noise, a desperate choke for release. Then he squeezed her tight and buried his face in her shoulder. "Sophia!"

She came again with him as he released himself inside her.

They panted and clung together. He didn't pull away, so she kept her legs anchored around him. A shudder ran through his torso as he touched his damp forehead to hers. Sophia found his face and smoothed her fingers over his jaw.

"Sorry," he said, winded. "Christ. I hadn't planned on going quite that far."

It took a moment for his words to sink in and when they did, Sophia giggled. "We're still on the clock." For some reason, that amused her more than it horrified.

"Don't remind me," Reed grumbled and rained kisses over her face before he pressed some kind of tissue into her hand. "It's a clean napkin I had in my pocket from the fast food I ordered at lunch."

"Oh. Bless you." As she cleaned herself, she flushed. "I was supposed to be looking for an empty filing cabinet."

"Want some help?" He tucked her blouse back into her skirt and then pulled away to assist her off the table.

"No. I'm finished looking anyway."

As soon as her feet touched the ground, her knees buckled. She grabbed for him in the dark and instantly he was there, supporting her.

He held her until she found her footing and could stand on her own. "Okay, now?"

"Yes, thank you." She tried to move away, but he was reluctant to let her go. "Uh, Reed?"

"Hmm?"

"You don't happen to have my underwear, do you?"

"Oh, hell. No."

She heard him move around, patting the floor. She tried the tabletop, but it seemed clear of debris. Just when she started to panic, he called, "Found them."

"Thank God." When he touched her ankle, she lifted a foot so he could put them on her. It felt odd to have someone else pulling her underwear up her legs. She flushed, thinking of how she'd just had sex with her heels on. Dear Lord, she'd had all her clothes on, except her panties.

She was glad it was too dark for Reed to see her stained cheeks. He snapped her panty band over her hips and took his time removing his hands from under her skirt.

"Thank you," she said, feeling her body heat again.

"No. Thank *you*." He kissed her, nuzzling her neck before he pulled away. "I used to hate the dark," he said. Then he inhaled the scent of her hair and added, "But not after that. I may just love it now." With a last quick caress to her cheek, he murmured, "Don't forget the meeting we all have with Marcus in fifteen minutes."

"What?" She frowned as his voice faded across the room. "Reed!"

"See you soon."

She heard the door open and soon light flooded the room. She winced and blinked. By the time she could see again, she was completely alone in the basement of Kendrick. She looked down her body and noticed he'd set her clothes back into neat order. Save for the wetness between her legs, the wadded napkin in her hand, and the tingling coursing through her entire body, Reed Walker had left no signs of recent lovemaking.

Footsteps overhead told her he was returning to accounting. Sophia smiled secretly. She shook her head and turned back toward the open filing cabinet she'd been inspecting. She'd pay the man back later for scrambling her up like this. And she'd have fun doing it.

CHAPTER 19

A week after his sexy escapade with Sophia in the basement of Kendrick, life felt like it was finally returning to normal. Better than normal. Reed couldn't have been happier or more content the evening she came over to fix his family lasagna with a fresh garden salad for supper and a cobbler pie for dessert.

Nic, being his usual annoying self, hovered as she cooked, flirting mercilessly. But Reed didn't mind since it made Sophia laugh, and he so loved her laugh. He couldn't take his eyes off her as he sat at the counter watching his roommate desperately try to work his mojo…and fail. Danni slid up onto a stool next to him and opened of her notebook to doodle.

Reed glanced over to watch her sketch a picture of Sophia cooking. Glad she was finally returning to more of the sister he remembered, he leaned toward her and smacked a quick kiss to her cheek.

Nic peered their way, popping his head up from over Sophia's shoulder where she was busy draining pasta water into the sink. "If this turns out any good, you can ditch Walker and run away with me, you know."

She laughed. "Why, thank you, Nic. It's always nice to have more options. But for now, I'm good. Thanks."

Still grinning at Reed as he spoke to her, Nic leaned against the counter. "And if this fellow here gives us any trouble, I can think up a few interesting ways to dispose of a body."

"Back off," Reed warned, but he felt too light-hearted to put much heat behind his tone.

Winking at him, Nic glanced once—conspiratorially—at Sophia's turned back before he snuck an extended finger toward her tomato sauce. But he never made it, because his hand got slapped.

"Ouch!" Gasping, he snapped his fingers back, his eyes wide as he glared. Rubbing his red knuckles, he sulked. "That hurt."

"Well, you deserved it," she said, only to slump her shoulders when he blinked his wounded, puppy dog stare at her. Shaking her head, she rolled her eyes. "Okay, fine. But don't stick your dirty fingers in my sauce."

Nic's brow shot up. "I wouldn't dare," he said, and grinned toward a still-scowling Reed.

Reed only sighed and shook his head, grateful Sophia was more entertained by his buffoon of a roommate than irritated.

She opened drawers, searching and rifling until she found a spoon, and dipped out a liberal sample of sauce. "Here," she offered.

"Thanks," Nic said, taking the spoon, and then went in quick for a hard kiss on her mouth. As he pulled back, he sent a smug look toward Reed. "Mmm. Your woman's not a bad kisser, Walker."

Reed glanced toward *his woman*. When she looked more baffled than insulted, he shook his head yet again. "Just remember, I know how to dispose of a body too, *pal*."

Nic laughed and popped the spoonful of Sophia's Eschell Special into his mouth, only to moan and roll his eyes into the back of his head. "Oh, dear Lord. Run away with me and marry me, Soph. Right now."

As she snorted and turned away to remove the sauce from the heat, Danni suddenly shut the sketchbook and looked up, making Reed jolt. He'd almost forgotten she was sitting next to him.

"I have an announcement," she said.

After Sophia sat her pasta down and Nic pulled the now-clean spoon from his mouth, Danni waited yet another moment, taking a deep breath. Reed's brow furrowed, wondering what was taking this much trouble to announce. It sounded big.

"I found a new place to live." When she paused, no one said a word in response. She turned to Reed, who for some reason felt as if someone had just thumped him in the solar plexus.

"I called the college today. I'm not going to wait until next semester to restart my classes. I think I can catch up. They've already found a new apartment for me to stay in and everything. Not a dorm room, but something with more privacy and security."

She nudged Reed's shoulder with hers. "So smile, big brother. You're finally getting your bed back."

When he didn't, her face fell. "What's wrong?"

He shook his head. "Nothing. It's just…are you sure you're ready for this?"

She nodded, her eyes bright. "Yes. I'm positive. I want to go back to school."

"Well, I say congratulations are in order then," Sophia broke in. She rushed to Danni and threw her arms around her. The two women hugged each other tightly.

When she pulled back, Danni turned right back to Reed with an uneasy wince.

He wasn't sure what was wrong with him. But his mouth was drawn tight, and his muscles were balled with tension. It felt too soon. He didn't think *he* was ready to let her go.

"I want to see this place first," he said before he pulled her into his own reluctant hug.

Nic stayed back. Reed suddenly noticed he was the only one who'd yet to say anything, a rare occurrence for Dominic Calhoun. He merely slipped his hands into his pockets and stood grimly by. When Danni turned to him, her eyes were expectant.

Nic's troubled gaze confused Reed as his friend looked

down at his hands and mumbled, "I can't believe you're leaving. I've gotten so used to seeing you every day."

"Well, I hope you come visit me occasionally," she said.

With a soft smile, he lifted his face. "Try to keep me away." He reached out to touch her hair.

Reed pulled back, a shock of intuition slamming into him as he watched his sister and roommate stare at each other with something much deeper than he'd ever noticed before.

As if sensing his surprise, Sophia wrapped her arm around his and rested her chin on his shoulder. "I'm so proud of how far you've come since the first time I met you, Danni. You're doing so well."

Danni blushed and glanced up at Nic as if she had him to thank for her progress, which sent off yet another alarm in Reed's head. What the hell was going on between those two?

"I've still got a ways to go," Danni murmured, her face glowing happily when Nic took her hand. "But, yeah, I think I'm progressing too."

"You know," Sophia drawled. "My dad is a psychologist if you ever think you need help."

Reed turned to Sophia in surprise.

Sophia smiled, her eyes completely on his sister. "He's the easiest person in the world to talk to. So if there's ever anything you want to talk about with a specialist—"

Reed cut her off sharply. "I thought you just said she was doing good."

Startled by his severe tone, Sophia spun to him. Her mouth fell open. "W-what?"

"I think it's a great idea," Nic said quietly. "I've always thought Danni needed some kind of professional counseling. Or maybe go to a group meeting."

"And *I've* always told you not to push it," Reed gritted out from between clenched teeth, whirling from Sophia to glare at his friend.

Nic narrowed his eyes. "Well, maybe you're wrong."

"Well, *maybe* you should just leave it be."

Nic threw his hands into the air. "Jesus, Walker. What's

your problem? If she wants more help—"

"She never *said* she wanted more help. And she's not ready yet. I don't want you *pressuring* her into anything, Calhoun."

"I'm not pressuring. I'm just saying—"

"Reed," Danni cut in softly. "I think...I think I would like to talk to a psychologist."

The fight hissing out of his body, Reed felt his face drain of color. He bobbed his head, which felt suddenly heavy on his neck. "If that's what you want, then fine." He knew his voice sounded harsh, but he couldn't help it. He was fraying at the seams.

"Reed?" Sophia said softly.

Her voice steadied him as nothing else could. He turned in her direction, and his eyes finally focused on her worried face. She set a hand on his arm.

Repeating his name, she asked, "What's wrong?"

He shook his head.

But she didn't buy it. "No. Talk to us. Why don't you want her to see a counselor?"

"I never said I didn't want her to talk to a counselor."

"Then—"

"If she wants help, that's fine. It's great." He sounded defensive though, so no one seemed to believe him.

"But there's something else bothering you," she insisted. "What is it?"

He merely shook his head and refused to meet her gaze.

"What are you afraid of?" Nic asked.

"Nothing," he muttered. Everything. God. Why did he feel so unstable all of the sudden? He thought he had things back under control, a carefully structured, orderly world. And then bam, lately chaos ruled without warning. He couldn't even seem to get a handle on his own freaking emotions.

"I've talked to my dad a little about this," Sophia said. "And before Danni can completely heal, she has to work out quite a few things. There are certain steps for recovering from rape."

Reed flinched at the word, and to his horror, he realized Danni did not. She merely turned to Sophia, listening intently.

"First, there's fear and shock. Disbelief. Then a woman turns to a form of denial. She just wants to forget and move on, even tries to do so. After pushing everything down, she gives off the impression that things are back to normal. But with her feelings restricted like that, she's far from normal. She still has to deal with it. A total flood of emotions will overflow next. Anger, depression, anxiety, a total loss of control. And then finally, once she works through *that*, she can begin to accept and move on."

Ah, Reed thought bitterly. No wonder he'd been a total fruit basket lately, unable to get a grip on his emotions. He was repressing too much. Good to know.

"So that explains it," Nic murmured, mirroring his thoughts.

He glanced up in time to catch his roommate turn to him with a glare. "You selfish son of a bitch," Nic hissed. "This isn't about Danni at all, is it? It's about *you*. You don't want her to go to a counselor to talk about what happened because you think she's going to reveal *your* little secret."

Reed sucked in a quick breath. His vision went black and for a second he feared he was going to pass out. But he blinked repeatedly until Nic's face came into focus.

"What're you talking about?" he asked softly.

Suddenly, his friend's eyes flared as if he'd just realized what he had said. Then his fierce features fell, and only compassion lingered in his eyes. Nic's dramatic change made the back of Reed's neck tickle with a frightening awareness. His stomach knotted painfully.

"She told me," Nic answered softly.

Reed's eyes swiveled to Danni. She covered her mouth with both hands; her eyes were large and frightened.

"You..." He tried to talk, but it felt like the air had been pummeled from his lungs. "You...remember?" he finally asked on a hoarse whisper.

She nodded. "I remember everything."

Reed swallowed. Blindly, he reached for the counter, some kind of stable support. Bile rose in his throat.

"And you told *him?*" he rasped in horror. "You told *Nic?*"

Tears prickled her eyes. "I'm sorry. I'm so sorry, Reed. I had to talk about it. I had to tell *someone.*"

He nodded in understanding, but his eyes burned, and a swirling sensation grew in his belly.

Oh, God. Oh, God. Nic *knew*. That was the one thing on earth he never wanted his roommate to know.

"Reed, man," Nic said softly, stepping toward him.

Reed stumbled away, holding up his hands to ward his friend off.

Nic stopped and nodded. "You're still my best friend. Nothing's ever going to change that."

Reed's vision faded. The swirling started up his esophagus. Soon, if it kept climbing, he was going to gag on it.

"Reed?" Sophia's soft, soothing voice reached him. He saw her at the fringes of his eyesight, reaching toward him. He pulled back, unable to be touched.

Immediate hurt crinkled her features.

He squeezed his eyes closed. "Sophia," he whispered in apology. "I'm sorry. I…"

God. He couldn't keep it together.

Running a hand through his hair, he spun away from the three worried faces of the most important people in his life.

"I have to get out of here."

He dashed toward the door.

~*~

Sophia hurried after him. She was completely in the dark about what was going on, but she sensed that it was bad. Reed didn't acknowledge her behind him except to mutter, "I'm not good company right now."

"I wasn't looking for good company. I just want to be with you, Reed."

He stormed down the stairs and out the front doors of his apartment building. "Just…leave me alone, okay? I need a little time here. I need *space.*"

But she continued to dog his heels. "Time and space for *what*? I have no idea what happened or what you and Nic and Danni were talking about. But whatever it was, it upset you. I'm worried about you."

"Well, *don't*. I'm fine."

"No, you're *not*."

He ignored her and kept walking.

Fed up, Sophia reached out and grabbed his arm, jerking him around. "Wake up, Reed," she snarled, glaring up at him. "I'm here for you."

A moaning sound came from his throat. He shook his head to deny it.

She reached for him and cupped his face with such a light touch. He bowed his head and closed his eyes, sinking closer to her.

"Talk to me," she murmured, reaching up to press her mouth against his. A deep whimper came from the back of his throat as their lips brushed together. His fingers tunneled through her hair; he gripped her scalp almost painfully as he buried himself into the kiss.

Just as Sophia tried to move closer, he suddenly ripped himself away, breathing hard.

"Damn it," he yelled as he fisted his hands and glared. "I said no! I need space. Just give me some space."

Her lips parted. But she didn't say a word. After staring at him a moment longer, she murmured "Fine."

Then she turned and walked away. She'd give him space. He could have all the freaking space he wanted. The stubborn, hard-headed buffoon. And if he ever wanted her back, he was going to have to crawl on hands and knees and beg for forgiveness because that was the rudest thing anyone had ever done to her.

CHAPTER 20

It was late when Reed returned to the apartment. Nic lingered in the kitchen, cleaning dishes and putting them away.

He glanced over as Reed slipped in the door. "Hey."

Reed met his gaze briefly before he had to drop his face. How was he ever going to look his roommate in the eye again? Trying to ignore Nic, he busied himself by emptying his pockets and piling his wallet and some change on the counter. Then he scooped it all up and headed toward his room. After depositing everything on his dresser, he frowned as he glanced toward his bed. Back in the living room, he glanced at the couch and then the bathroom door, which was hanging open.

"Where's Danni?"

"She's asleep," Nic said, drying off the last plate and slipping it onto a cabinet shelf.

"But she's not in my room."

"No," Nic answered. He met Reed's questioning gaze and he sent him a level stare.

"Then where..." His words died off as he glanced at Nic's closed bedroom door. Gaze zipping to his roommate, he could instantly tell the truth. The realization that his sister was asleep in Nic's bed almost knocked him to his knees.

"You got a problem with that?" Nic murmured.

Reed wasn't sure. Suddenly everything started to pile on him; he couldn't take the pressure. Sophia was gone. Danni was with Nic. And his best friend knew his worst secret ever.

"I need a smoke," he muttered.

He barreled to the window, threw it open, and climbed out onto the fire escape. Nic followed. He leaned outside and watched Reed. A cold breeze washed in around them as Reed lit his cigarette. He blew out a cloud of smoke and paced the short length of the escape. He wasn't wearing a coat, but he didn't feel the chill.

Reed took another drag before glaring toward Nic, who'd sat down in the open window ledge, patiently waiting for his friend's response. "She's not one of your play toys, Calhoun."

"I know."

Reed pointed a glowing tip at him. "I'm not going to let you turn her into one."

"I won't either." Nic's voice became defensive.

Tossing the hardly smoked cigarette over the side, Reed growled. "She's vulnerable right now. How could you take advantage of her like that? You, of all people, should know what she's been through."

"That's right," Nic snapped. "I do know what she's been through. I'm not the Big Bad Wolf, Walker. And she's not Little Red Riding Hood. Just look at how far she's come. That woman's a lot stronger than she looks. She's...she's amazing."

Reed's jaw dropped. "Oh, my God. You're in love with her."

Nic gave a bitter laugh, grabbed the top of the open window, and said, "I'm not sure how it happened."

"It's Danni," Reed said.

Nic grinned. "Enough said."

Reed sat on the edge of the fire escape's railing, stunned. "Have you told her yet?"

Nic sighed. "No. I've still been trying to get used to the idea myself."

"So did you guys, you know, do...anything?"

Nic's eyes shot to Reed's. "What? You want details?"

Reed grimaced. "God, no. I just wondered if Danni *could*, you know…after what happened. I didn't think she'd want anyone to ever touch her again."

Nic smiled wistfully. "All we did was kiss, but she did wonderfully. I think I was more nervous than she was. I couldn't keep my hands still."

He looked down at his hands as if to check and see if they were still shaking, and then looked up at Reed. "I couldn't stop worrying if she could feel the tremors. I don't…I'm not sure if she thought about the rape, or how much it bothered her. But I couldn't get it out of my head. I kept thinking, 'Did he touch her here too?' Was I going to do something he'd done and trigger a bad memory?" He fisted his hands suddenly.

"She was so soft and small and weaker than me. But she looked up at me with so much trust in her eyes. How could some monster take that and break it? I wanted to go out and hunt him down so I could snap every bone in his body. But I also wanted to stay there and protect her. I almost freaking cried, I was so scared of doing something to make her afraid of me."

He covered his mouth with one of his fists. Reed stood and went to him. He sat a hand on Nic's shoulder and squeezed. Nic looked up. This was his roommate, his best friend, the man he could tell anything. It'd been too long since they'd just traded stories. Reed suddenly missed the release of tension he always got when he unloaded his thoughts on Nic. He was glad to have that back.

"I almost cried," Nic repeated. "When she needed me to be strong and confident, I almost bawled all over your little sister. And all we did was *kiss*."

Reed patted and then let go of Nic's shoulder. "Yeah, you always were a little sissy baby."

Nic stared up at him, dumbfounded, and then both men broke out into grins. "Jack ass," Nic said, and dove out the window at Reed's legs to tackle him. But Reed dodged to one side and Nic landed on the freezing floor of the fire escape, getting a face full of cold, wet metal. As he stared down between the bars at the alley twenty feet below, the escape creaked and swayed under him. Reed grabbed the railings for support and Nic tried to brace himself on his hands and knees.

"Smooth move, Calhoun," Reed said, his voice a bit unsteady. "Get us both killed."

"Holy hell," Nic choked out, still trying to gain his equilibrium on the swaying aperture. "How can you come out here all the time?"

Reed grabbed Nic's arm, hauling him to his feet. "What? Are you afraid of heights?"

Nic grabbed the side as he stared at the street below. "Didn't used to be." He was still a bit hoarse. Finally, he steadied himself and came away from the edge. "It's cold enough." He rubbed his arms and glanced down at the mess the wet metal had made of his clothes. He scrambled back for the window.

But Reed stopped him. "Hey. Thank you."

Nic looked up. Reed knew the gratitude in his gaze was unmistakable, but Nic still had to be a smart aleck about it. "For what? Making out with your sister?"

Reed's jaw clenched, but then he eased. "Actually, I think you're exactly what Danni needs."

Looking suddenly very sober, Nic rasped, "I hope so."

Reed nodded his assurance. "You are. And you were right about me. I was...I've been running away from this."

"No." Nic shook his head in denial.

"Yes," Reed argued. "I didn't know how to deal with it, didn't know what to do."

Nic slapped a hand on Reed's back. "Come on, this is Danni we're talking about. She ended up taking care of us two."

Reed smiled, the pride of an adoring brother filling him as he thought about how accomplished his Danni had turned out.

"So how did things go with Sophia?" Nic's voice broke in, making him close his eyes. "You didn't tell her, did you?"

Reed didn't bother to shake his head. He couldn't manage to look at Nic. His stomach muscles tightened; he wished the moment away. He'd never, *never* wanted Nic to know.

"Reed," Nic said softly. "Man, you're my best friend. I love you like a brother. Nothing that happened to you when you were twelve is going to change that." Reed didn't answer. So Nic kept talking. "Why didn't you ever tell me? We tell each other everything."

Finally, Reed glanced over. "Would you have talked about it?"

That question seemed to catch his friend off guard. Nic thought about it a moment before he finally shrugged. Solemnly, he admitted, "No, probably not."

Reed sighed. He blinked a few times and filled his nose with the crisp breeze.

"It was pretty awful, huh?" Nic asked quietly.

"Yeah."

"I never understood why you were so close to Danni, why you were so protective. I mean, sure, she was your sister and as her big brother, you felt some responsibility. But you always took it so far. I didn't get it. I'm sorry."

Reed didn't want to think about his past. He didn't want to think, period. But there was so much going on inside his head. And Nic wanted to talk. Why did everyone always want to freaking talk?

Jesus, fine. He'd talk. He blew out a breath. "I'm in love with her."

Out of the corner of his eye, he saw Nic turn his way. "Sophia?" At Reed's nod, Nic snorted. "Let me guess. You didn't tell her that either."

Reed shook his head. "I don't know how. She's the bright part of my whole day. She makes me think there is such a thing as happily ever after, like everything that's ever happened before now doesn't matter, and that…" His voice turned hoarse so he gave up on talking for a moment. "I want too much when I'm with her." He glanced at Nic. "Things this good just don't happen to me. I feel like if I let her be with me, then she'll just get sucked down into the darkness right along with me. I'm sure I've already got everyone at the office gossiping about her like she's some kind of—"

"Oh, will you can it already with the pity party? You're getting a little too dramatic there, princess."

Reed's jaw tightened as he glared at Nic. "Never mind," he muttered. "You couldn't understand. You have no idea what any of this is like for me."

"You're right. I don't know. I can't imagine what kind of hell you grew up in, Reed. I don't even want to. All I know is that you're one amazing person to overcome it and get to where you are today. Just look at yourself, will you? You're a successful accountant with a drop-dead gorgeous girlfriend, a sister who's sweeter than anything you deserve, and a roommate who is off the charts amazing." He grinned a little at his last comment.

"You're not that twelve-year-old boy anymore. You're a grown man, and you're safe now. Your world is good. So don't let something like Sophia slip through your fingers because you think your past is going to come after you. It won't."

"What about what happened to Dan—"

"What happened was tragic, but it has nothing to do with your childhood. Atrocities will happen no matter who you are. And don't think that something couldn't happen to Sophia just because you stay away from her."

Reed lifted his face.

"She could get hurt without you there just as easily as she could *with* you there."

Reed didn't answer, but he didn't need to. Nic had gotten his point across. He shook his head, wondering when his goofball roommate had turned into a genius.

Nic tapped the front of Reed's shoulder with a fist. "Now let's get inside before I freeze my balls off."

CHAPTER 21

Reed strode down the halls of Kendrick, his attention buried in a file and his mind miles away, when he heard his name called.

"Hey, Walker."

He glanced up to discover Sophia and two of her coworkers flagging him down.

His heart beat hard through his pulse as he slowed to a stop. She was so beautiful it made his chest burn. He hadn't talked to her since pushing her away two days ago, didn't know what to say, wasn't sure if he should even try. The fact that she'd avoided him in return told him it was probably best for her to move on without him. He wasn't too sure if he could move on without her, however.

She looked annoyed while the two men on either side of her wore somewhat cocky expressions.

"We need your help deciding something," the man to call his name spoke up.

Reed studied Sophia's face for a moment, then slid his gaze to Zack Braddock, the guy on her right. "What's the problem?"

Zack waved a folder in front of his face, and Reed took it from his hand. "We're having trouble figuring out who should take this case."

Reed only had to examine the name of the account to understand why workers would fight over it. It was a commissioned job. That meant it was top priority and whoever took on the assignment of overseeing it would get a special bonus. The amount of that bonus varied on how much money the project turned over. These cases were few and far between, but when one came around, people leapt on it like a group of freezing men to a struck match.

Reed looked up and handed it to Sophia. "Take care of this."

He watched her exhale with relief as she smiled. "Thank you." She took the file from him and threw her coworkers a triumphant smirk.

Reed turned away and started back down the hall before he heard the muted words, "Boy, I wish *I* was sleeping with Walker too, so I could get a commissioned account."

As his footsteps came to a grinding halt, Reed pivoted slowly back around. The first thing he saw was Sophia's expression. She looked pissed, but not quite as pissed as he felt.

She was the only one who noticed him striding back to the group. As her gaze met his, she sucked in a breath and took a step back. Reed could only guess how much of the rage he felt was mirrored on his face. Zack caught her reaction but didn't even have time to glance up before Reed grabbed the punk by his upper arm and spun him around.

"What did you say?"

Zack's Adam's apple bobbed in his throat. "Noth-nothing."

"No," Reed shook his head. "I definitely heard you say something."

"It wasn't important."

"Oh, I think it was."

Frightened eyes shifted to his cohort, but the other guy was already taking off down the hall and barely sent him a final I'm-getting-the-hell-out-of-Dodge look before he disappeared around a cubicle. The big-mouth glanced up to Reed uneasily. "Look, I didn't mean to offend—"

Reed pushed him against the wall.

By his throat.

Sophia gasped. Suddenly, she was there, gripping his arm and trying to pull him away. "Reed, just leave it be."

Reed gave her a look that would have sent anyone else fleeing. It even had her letting go of his arm and taking a step back. But her eyes continued to plead. "Reed," she begged in a desperate, quiet voice.

He studied her for a moment as if debating her request. Then he shook his head in denial before turning his attention back to Zack, who he held pinned against the wall. He just couldn't let this slide. "Tell me," he said in an oddly casual voice, given the circumstances. "Who's been dealing with this client for the past five months?"

Zack swallowed. Reed could feel the convulsive movement of an esophagus working against his palm.

"Eschell," he rasped, risking a quick glance toward Sophia.

"Good," Reed encouraged. "And *who* assigned that task to her?"

Closing his eyes briefly, Zack opened them to stare directly at Reed. "Marcus," he admitted.

Reed let go of the throat, and its owner gulped in air greedily until his face lost its redness. But Reed wasn't nearly finished with him. "So why wouldn't I give her the account, since she knows their history a lot better than you or your little dipshit friend?"

"I don't know, sir."

Reed nodded as if he understood Zack's predicament. "Then I think you owe Miss Eschell an apology." He made it sound like it was the only reasonable solution to a complex problem.

Zack looked to Sophia briefly and then away as if he feared staring at her too long might heighten Reed's rage. "I'm sorry, Sophia. I'm so sorry."

Pressing a hand against her forehead, Sophia closed her eyes and nodded her forgiveness.

Reed wasn't so satisfied though. Stepping close, he warned, "Don't ever let me hear you saying anything like that again."

He watched the asshole's head bob before Zack took a step back so he could slink from between Reed and the wall and escape down the hall. Reed glared after him before he veered his gaze to Sophia.

Her jaw was as hard as granite. The flush covering her face wasn't from fear or embarrassment. The fire blazing in her brown eyes came from pure anger, and he felt sorry for putting her on the spot. But she was *his* woman, and he wasn't about to stand by and let some loser treat her like the office slut, especially because of him.

As if to apologize, he said, "That wasn't something I could ignore."

"We'll discuss it later," she gritted out. Then she turned her back to him and took her file with her as she stalked away.

Reed clenched his teeth. Or they could discuss it now. He had missed her these past few days. And right now, he had to be near her just a little longer. Even if it was to argue.

Ignoring the heads poking out of their cubicles and taking in a week's worth of gossip, he stormed after his woman.

~*~

As Sophia fumed down the hall, she felt Reed hot on her heels.

He'd nearly choked an employee to death. Because of her. Okay, maybe "to death" was a little too harsh. But Reed had murder in his eyes when he'd pushed Zack Braddock against the wall. It scared her.

He couldn't go around just choking people willy-nilly. He was going to get himself fired. And it was all because he didn't want gossip spread about their relationship.

Sophia had to admit, she wasn't too sure what to think about that. Sure, she could see why he wouldn't want to be the topic of hot gossip around the water cooler, but the fact that he was so averse to the idea of being labeled her boyfriend kind of hurt. What was wrong with her that he didn't want anyone to know they were together?

"I'm not going to apologize," he said.

Sophia slowed to a stop before she turned to look at him. His face was dark with color. She couldn't tell if it was anger, embarrassment, or what.

"Fine," she said calmly. "Just don't do it again."

"Don't..." He choked on her demand. "That's not a possibility either."

Sophia clenched her teeth. "Reed." She sighed. "Fine. Let's talk about it. But in your office."

"Fine." He followed her down the hallway of cubicles, past a bug-eyed Myrna, and into his office. Once he shut the door, she exploded.

"What the hell, Reed! Everyone here knows about us, okay? It's not something to choke a man over."

Reed blinked and stared at her. "I don't care who *knows*. That doesn't mean they all have to talk about you like you're some kind of..." He couldn't continue.

Sick of his caveman attitude, Sophia growled, "That gives you no reason to go around bullying people."

"I'll bully *anyone* who says anything negative against you."

She snorted. "I'm not some damsel in distress. I'm a big girl, and I can take care of myself." When Reed turned away to run his hand through his hair, she slapped a palm on the top of his desk. He sent her a sharp glance, but she glowered right back. "If I was worried about gossip, I never would've become involved with you in the first place."

He blinked. His eye were so full of emotion she ached to know what he was thinking. But he wasn't going to tell her. He never told her what was really going on in his mind.

"You could get fired for what you did today. My God, Reed. You assaulted a man. You could go to jail."

"I don't care," he bit out harshly. "I'd do the same thing if it happened again. He had no right to say that to you."

Sophia pressed a hand to her head and let out a growl of frustration, unable to take any more. "How can you just stand there and think that way? What you did was wrong. Wrong!"

He simply stared at her, his jaw locked as tight as his

stubborn pride.

She let out a snort of disgust and muttered, "I give up," as she turned away.

"Sophia," he said in alarm. He hurried after her and slapped his hand against the door before she could open it. "Sophia."

"I'm done," she said. "Let me out."

"Sophia," he said again, his voice raspy and pleading. "Don't...Please don't shut me out."

She gasped in outrage. "Shut *you* out? Don't you get it, Reed? You're the one shutting me out. That's the entire problem. You never really tell me what's going on with you. You just demand space and then ignore me for days on end."

He leaned forward and pressed his face to her shoulder blade. "What do you want me to say?"

She closed her eyes and tried to block out the pain emanating off him. Refusing to turn around or she might slip up and let him in again, she growled, "I want you to tell me what's really bothering you."

"Nothing," he whispered.

Her eyes snapped open.

Nothing? Ha! Nothing her lily white butt.

Poking her elbow backward into his stomach, she growled. "Let me out. Now." She didn't want to be in the lousy liar's company one second longer.

He grunted at the sharp prod but stayed his ground. "Soph—"

"No," she hissed. "Don't you dare stand there and tell me nothing's wrong. I saw your face, Reed. When you realized Nic and Danni both knew what your big secret was, you were devastated. Something is definitely wrong. And it's making you totally lose control of yourself."

He began to shake; she felt his tremors reverberate through her. "You want me to start dragging all my skeletons out of the closet. Is that it?" He jerked back, taking a step away from her. "Fine. Then sit down and shut up. I'll tell you every gory detail about the real Reed Walker."

Offended by the sneer in his tone, Sophia turned and tightly crossed her arms over her chest. "Fine," she grumbled right back, not moving an inch toward the chair he oh-so-rudely told her to take.

He paced the room and glared at the floor as he muttered, "I had my fucking life in *order*. Everything was going the way I wanted it to go. And then—"

"Yeah, yeah," Sophia muttered, breaking in. "Then I came along and messed up everything. I got it."

He paused to pierce her with an irritated glower. "That's not what I was going to say. Don't put words into my mouth, God damn it. If you want to hear this, *don't* interrupt." He cursed and yanked a hand through his hair. "I don't want to talk about it, and I'm not going to repeat it again. So listen and listen good, sweetheart. This is all you're going to get from me."

His tone of his voice, his demeaning attitude, his overall abrasive behavior piqued her beyond return.

Fisting her hands down at her sides, she glowered right back. "You know what. I don't even want to hear your precious little secret anymore. If it's that big of a deal, don't bother."

"It *is* that big of a deal," he roared. "But you're a bigger deal to me. And if you felt anything for me like what I feel for you, then you wouldn't make me talk about this. Jesus Christ, why do you have to know everything about my life anyway?"

Sophia's back stiffened with righteous indignation. "If that's some kind of declaration of love from you, then save it. Because if you really loved me like you claim you do, then you would've already told me everything important there was to tell. And this is obviously important, because it just broke us up."

Reed's face crumpled, but he didn't apologize, and he didn't start spilling his guts.

She snorted and rolled her eyes. "God. I am *so* through with men." Pivoting back toward the door, she opened it and slammed it closed on her way out.

CHAPTER 22

Dropping into his desk chair, Reed buried his face in his hands as all his anger drained. He had bungled things. Badly. God, what had he been thinking? He'd just lost Sophia. He was going to grow old alone, a miserable, pathetic heap unless—

He had to tell her. Everything. That's all there was to it. And he had to remain calm when he did.

He cracked off an incredulous laugh. Calm? He couldn't even remain calm when he *thought* about it. His hands were already shaking and a sick, cold sweat slithered down the back of his neck. But throwing up protective walls by becoming irate and irritable had definitely not worked just now when he'd been ready to spill all. It had only made Sophia defensive and equally upset to the point she didn't even want to listen to him.

He took a deep breath when his lungs began to contract with the hint of hyperventilation. Calm, he reminded himself. Just. Calm. Down.

His intercom beeped. "Mr. Walker?" Myrna spoke with a hesitant voice.

He lifted his face, frowning over the fact she'd just called him Mr. Walker and not Reed. "Yes?"

"I, uh, I'm sorry to bother you, but…Mr. Kendrick wants to see you in his office. Right away."

"Oh, shit." Closing his eyes, he wiped a hand over his brow. He'd totally forgotten about pinning Zack Braddock to the wall by his throat. "Thank you, Myrna."

Standing, he straightened his jacket, smoothed down his tie, then checked his hair in the reflection of the glass out his office window. No one else needed to know how out of sorts he felt or that he was on his way to the big office to be fired.

But maybe a pink slip was not in his future. Maybe he'd only be suspended. Kendrick liked him. Maybe he still had a chance.

As he left his office and strode purposefully down the hall, however, his hopes dimmed as every employee he passed grew wide-eyed and dodged to the side, giving him plenty of berth.

He couldn't help but go the route past Sophia's workspace. Thankfully, she hadn't heard the rumors yet, otherwise he doubted she'd still be seated at her desk with her back to the cubicle opening as she typed at her keyboard and studied her computer screen with her new commissioned file open in her lap.

The muscles around his heart gripped painfully. She was so beautiful, sitting there, her back straight and feminine, her strawberry blond hair falling over her shoulders. He wondered if this was the last time he'd ever see her just like this, or if it was the last time he'd ever see her at all.

Moving on, he waited until he was alone in the elevator before he tried to clear the knot out of his throat. It didn't work. He patted at his jacket again with cold, trembling fingers.

When the doors slid open, admitting him to the top floor, he paused a moment, loath to exit the security of the elevator. Shaking his head, he forced himself forward. This was just a job—the best job he'd ever had, but still…just a paycheck. He had survived through worse; he could survive through this.

The last twenty feet to the receptionist's desk outside the double doors of Kendrick's inner sanctum felt like the walk of doom. His last mile.

And Mrs. Drew's usual smile for him was not in place. "Go on in, Mr. Walker," she said, her eyes sympathetic. "They're already waiting for you."

They?

He nodded and took a deep breath.

Inside, he wasn't surprised to find Zack Braddock smirking up at him from the chair seated across Kendrick's desk from Mr. Kendrick himself. But Marcus pacing along the side of the room caught him off guard.

Marcus paused and lifted his head. Pointing toward the CEO, he demanded, "Tell them this is ridiculous."

With a tired sigh, Kendrick ran his hand over his face and leaned back in his chair. "Marcus," he muttered. "Sit down."

"But——"

"*Sit down.*" When his brother-in-law regretfully flopped into a chair, Kendrick motioned toward Reed. "You, too."

Quietly, Reed took the last remaining seat. When he perched himself stiffly on the edge, Kendrick sighed again. His eyes were weary as he regarded Reed.

"Mr. Braddock claims you tried to strangle him down in accounting just now. Is this true?"

Prepared to take his punishment like a big boy, Reed braced every muscle in his body and nodded. "Yes. I pinned him to the wall by his throat until he agreed to apologize to a coworker for something offensive he said to her."

"See." Marcus jerked to his feet, jabbing his finger in Reed's direction. "He was just defending Sophia. He shouldn't——"

This time, Kendrick didn't even bother to speak. He merely sent his kin a speaking look, and the pear-shaped man snapped his jaw shut and slumped back into his chair.

Reed, however, was in shock. He hadn't expected Marcus to defend him. He thought Weatherby would be excited to see him go. Then again, Marcus would no longer have anyone around to take on his responsibilities.

Reed's gut burned. Ah hell, he was even going to miss doing Marcus's job for him.

Veering his gaze back to Reed, Kendrick studied him quietly before saying, "My hands are tied here, Reed. Physical assault on a coworker cannot be tolerated. Mr. Braddock has agreed not to file criminal charges against you, but I can't even let you off with a warning. No suspension, no two-weeks' notice. Your employment with Kendrick is terminated immediately."

Nodding and using all the control he possessed to keep his face bland of expression, Reed murmured, "I understand, sir."

Inside, his body crumpled.

He might've known it was coming, but hearing the actual words made his ears ring. His mouth was so dry he licked his lips twice before giving up the fruitless effort of trying to wet them.

Apology thick in his gaze, Kendrick finished gently, "We'll give you two weeks' severance pay and an hour to clear out your office."

Another nod was all Reed could manage. After a difficult swallow, he rasped, "What about Braddock's punishment? His treatment toward Ms. Eschell is grounds for sexual harassment."

If he was going down, he was going to take the smirking, loud-mouthed smartass with him.

Kendrick nodded once. "Marcus has fully explained what happened, and Mr. Braddock has agreed to apologize to her. But I'm sorry, Reed. Miss Eschell hasn't come forward to press the issue. And I'm disinclined to file a formal complaint against him at this time." He lifted his hands as if to show that they were metaphorically tied. "How do you think I talked him out of pressing charges against you?"

Reed felt like weeping. He could handle being fired for his part. But no justice for Sophia made his blood boil. "I think I'd rather go to jail."

Kendrick folded his hands calmly, a slight smile cracking his lips. "Well, I happen to like you, Reed, so I negotiated on your behalf. It's not up to you."

Nodding, Reed pushed to his feet.

"Thank you for coming to Kendrick Advertising," Kendrick murmured, looking like he might start crying too. "You will be missed."

As Reed turned away, Zack caught his eye and smirked up at him from his comfortable lounge in his padded chair. When he waved a few fingers in farewell, Reed snapped.

Fisting his hand, he reared back his arm and slammed his knuckles into the smug bastard's nose, making Braddock's chair tip over backwards and spill him onto the floor.

"Reed!" Kendrick screamed as he surged to his feet. "What the hell?"

Feeling loads better, Reed shrugged and sent his old CEO apologetic wince. "If he was going to get me fired for physical assault I thought he should at least look assaulted. And hell, I might as well throw in a death threat while I'm at it."

Turning back to watch Zack clutching his bloody nose as he scrambled to pick himself up off the carpet, Reed pointed an ominous finger. "Mess with her again, and I'll come back to finish you off."

With that, he strolled from Kendrick's office smoothing his hands down his unwrinkled suit jacket as he went.

CHAPTER 23

Propping a single cardboard box against his hip and holding it with one arm so he could dig out his apartment key, Reed felt surprisingly calm.

Then again, when a person hit rock bottom, he had to feel somewhat grounded with the secure knowledge there was no lower he could fall. He could only climb up from here.

Shrugging his way into the brightly lit kitchen, Reed noticed he was not alone.

"I don't know what's worse," he said, dropping his personal effects from Kendrick onto the kitchen bar. The box slapped against the countertop when it landed, gaining the attention of the couple snuggling on the couch. "The fact that I lost my job, lost the girl, or that my best friend is now dating my little sister."

Both Danni and Nic surged to their feet.

"You lost your job?"

"You lost Sophia?"

Tugging off his tie, he tossed it into the box with the rest of three years' worth of crap. "Yep. Yep. And…yep."

Danni started toward him, "Oh, my God, Reed. What happened?"

For some reason, the worry in her wide eyes made him smile. Gathering her into an enveloping hug, he buried his face in her hair and inhaled the scent of her shampoo, grateful she'd come so far since her attack.

"I don't really want to talk about it right now." Pulling back and keeping his hands clasped around the sides of her shoulders, he held her at arm's length as he studied her face. "Was Nic right? Am I the reason you haven't gone to therapy yet?"

She blinked, clearly not prepared for the sudden change in conversation. "What?"

"Don't ever let me hold you back, Danni. If you have to talk about it, then talk about. Do whatever you need to do to heal. Okay? And don't worry about me. I'll survive."

Hell, he might just have that sentiment tattooed to his ass. Bring out Gloria Gaynor and cue the music because Reed Walker was going to survive.

"But—"

He cut her off by hauling her back to his chest for another bone-crushing hug. After drawing away, he kissed her forehead and turned toward Nic, yanking him into an equally enormous embrace. His roommate got the same treatment with a quick peck to the forehead.

Nic jerked back in surprise, confusion apparent on his face. "Dude."

"Hurt my sister, and you die," Reed said since making death threats had become his thing today. Then he turned from both of them and started toward the window.

Nic grabbed his arm, looking alarmed. "Whoa. Where're you going?"

Reed pointed to his destination. "Onto the fire escape."

Just as Nic tightened his grip, Danni leapt forward and clutched his other arm.

Frowning, he glanced from one worried face to the other. "What?" Then he rolled his eyes. "Jesus, I'm not going to jump."

"Then why're you going out there?" Nic demanded, not

slackening his hold.

"To *think*," Reed answered, yanking his arm free. "For fresh air. To get away from watching you two neck on my couch. Christ, ease up. I need a moment alone."

"But——" Nic tried one more time.

Reed lifted his hand. "Just give me half an hour to mourn the loss of my old life. Then, when I come back, we'll talk business. Okay?"

His roommate's face crinkled into confusion. "Business?"

"Yeah." Reed nodded as if he'd planned this all along, when actually, the idea just hit him as he spoke. "You're going to quit Delta, and the two of us are going to start our own advertising firm together. Then Danni's going to head our art department once she graduates college in the spring."

"Really?" both his sister and roommate gasped together, their faces lighting with instant enthusiasm.

"Yes!" Nic cheered, pumping a fist into the air. "It's about damn time you came around. We're going to build the best freaking advertising firm ever."

"And you want me to join too?" Danni whispered, covering her mouth with her hands, tears of happiness gathering in her lashes.

"Hell, yes, we want you aboard," Nic answered before Reed could speak. When she squealed with excitement, Nic pressed a hard kiss to her mouth and spun her in a circle. "The three of us are going to make a kickass team. With Reed covering finances and legal mumbo-jumbo, you and I can focus on the cool, creative stuff, and there'll be no stopping us."

As the two of them continued jabbering, already arguing over a name for their new venture, Reed smiled softly. Nic and Danni didn't even notice when he turned away and shuffled like a tired, old man toward the fire escape.

He pulled himself out into the cold evening and welcomed the icy slap of breeze in his face, waking him to his new reality.

~*~

Sophia slowed to a stop when she rounded the corner on the sidewalk and Reed's building came into view. When she glanced up, the breath snagged in her chest. There he sat, all alone, on the fire escape with his back to the cold brick wall of the apartment complex and his feet stretched out in front of him. He'd lowered his dark head as he studied something in his lap.

Sophia's heart pounded painfully.

He looked so sad.

All the anger she'd felt earlier in his office drained out of her. She couldn't hate Reed Walker. Obviously, since she couldn't even stay mad at him, or even stay *away* from him.

She was destined to follow the generations of women before her and fall for a wounded, tortured hero. Though to tell the truth, her mother was quite happy with her father. And her grandma was happy too. As were her sisters. They really did love their men with deep, troubled problems. And they'd stayed with them all these years. That couldn't just be sympathy. It had to be real. It had to be love.

But how did she know if it was real with Reed? Still watching him from the ground as she drew closer, she noticed the object consuming his attention was a pack of cigarettes. Instead of bringing one to his lips and lighting up, he studied it a moment before tearing it in half, then into fourths, before flinging the broken pieces over the guardrail into the alley. After pulling out another cigarette, he repeated the process.

Sophia halted. She couldn't seem to breathe. Oh, God. He'd just overcome smoking. He'd conquered a bad habit.

Suddenly, she understood everything in clear, neon, blinking lights. It wasn't the torrid pasts that had seduced her mother and her grandmother and all her sisters to their irresistible yet angst-ridden men. It was the men themselves, men with backbone and strength who could live through hell and still make it out alive. Men who survived and triumphed.

Realizing Reed was one of those unique men, Sophia made her decision. And she felt completely confident about it. She loved Thaddeus Reed Walker, and she wasn't ready to give up on him after all.

Putting her fingers to her lips, she whistled loud and piercing.

His head jerked up. She waved to get his attention. He dropped the cigarette pack and fumbled to his feet, making the entire escape sway under him.

Her pulse jumped in her throat as she watched, but he merely braced his feet and grabbed hold of the railing to steady himself.

She smiled wide. Yep, a survivor.

"I'm coming up," she yelled, cupping her hands around her mouth before she pointed to the front door of his building.

He nodded and turned to disappear back into the window of his apartment.

Leaping into action, Sophia dashed toward the entrance. Loving the cold wind on her cheeks and the crisp breeze in her lungs, she rushed toward her destination: Reed.

~ * ~

Reed almost clunked his head on the top of the window frame in his haste to climb back inside. But Sophia was coming. His blood danced through his veins, the anxiety and excitement making his heart pump vigorously.

Danni and Nic must've stayed worried about him because they were lingering close to the window. Popping to his feet as Reed hurled himself into the apartment, Nic opened his mouth, but Reed was quicker.

"Get out," he panted. "Both of you." When Danni blinked, he lifted a hand and added for her benefit, "Sorry, but Sophia's coming up. I need to talk to her. Alone."

Nic's face darkened. "Sophia?" he muttered. Spinning on his heel, he stormed to the door and yanked it open just as a winded Sophia lifted her hand to knock. "You've got a lot of nerve showing your face here."

"*Hey*," Reed hollered, stalking forward just as he heard Sophia exclaim, "Excuse me?"

"How could you dump my boy on the same day he was fired?"

Reed was about to grab his roommate's shoulder and haul him out of her way when Sophia poked Nic in the chest with a long painted fingernail. "For your information, *pal*, I didn't know he'd been fired until a few minutes ago. So, what do you think I'm doing here right now?"

There was a pause and then Nic's voice was uncertain as he answered, "Oh. Well...in that case, you two should probably talk."

Sophia folded her arms over her chest and glared. "You think?"

Duly put in his place, Nic shifted to the side and let her in. When she saw Reed, she pulled up short.

He sent his roommate a look. "What was that?"

Nic shrugged ruefully, his cheeks coloring. "What? I was trying to defend you."

"Yeah," Reed muttered, rolling his eyes. "You can go now."

Danni swept forward. "Come on, Dominic." she hooked her arm through his. "Let's leave these two alone." She led him into the hallway and shut the door behind them.

Immediately, a thick silence rang around the apartment. Bolstering his courage, Reed met Sophia's gaze. Her brown eyes were glossy with unshed tears. She opened her mouth and said nothing.

He smiled. "I hoped you would come."

She sniffed and wiped at her cheek. "I'm so sorry, Reed. You were fired because of me. No matter what happened between us, this wasn't fair to you at all. I'm going to talk to Zack and get your job back. I swear, I'll——"

He shook his head. "I don't want my job back."

"——find a way to make this...what?" She blinked. "Why don't you want your job back? You love your job."

"Meh." He shrugged. "Nic and Danni and I are going to start up our own firm. I've got some money in my savings and..." His smile was crooked and light. "Want to join us? It's a totally risky venture that will probably fail in the first six month, not to mention suck up all your time and energy. But we'd love to include you."

Sophia studied him a moment before she huffed out a breath. "I need to sit down."

He moved aside and let her pass. As she settled deep into the seat of an armchair, he took the couch a couple feet away. She looked rattled. It was adorable. But then, every expression to cross Sophia Eschell's face held its own special charm.

When she didn't look like she could speak, he decided to start the dreaded discussion himself. "I know I've been a mess. And I am so sorry for the way I treated you today. Ever since Danni's attack, I haven't been able to get a grip on my life. But I can't...I can't push it down any longer. I can't forget it. I never will. And I realize now that I can't try to ignore it either. Nor can I keep it from you because you need to know what I'm dealing with. I refuse to lose you because of this."

Pressing her hand to her chest, Sophia licked her lips. "I haven't been fair to you, Reed. If you don't want to talk about it, whatever it is, I'll respect that. It's okay."

She was so beautiful; he could only stare at her lovely, compassionate face. Secure in the knowledge she would only be a font of support once the truth was out, he took a deep breath and admitted, "Talking about this isn't easy for me."

She nodded with a half-smile. "Yeah. I've caught on to that by now."

He sighed and rubbed at his face. "Actually, talking about it is impossible because I haven't. Not ever. Danni was there and she told Nic, so...." He shrugged. There was no one left to tell. Except Sophia. "I've been skimming through some of Danni's, uh, help pamphlets, and I guess you're supposed to talk to at least one person about...about your...experience. I want that person to be you. So you can't give me an out. You have to listen because I don't think I could tell anyone else."

Her shoulders heaved as she took a deep breath. But she seemed to brace herself because she straightened her back and nodded. "Okay. I'm ready to listen then. I won't interrupt, and I swear I won't get defensive and snippety this time."

"And I won't get pissy and rude," he promised.

When she smiled, he closed his eyes and leaned his head back, resting his skull against the sofa cushions. He could tell her. He could tell her and survive.

"So what did you want to tell me?"

He opened his eyes and tried to smile. "Since Danni's attack, I've had a hard time dealing with everything. It wasn't—" He stopped himself, not sure where he was trying to go with his words. So he cleared his head and started fresh. "I never knew who my father was. I doubt Joan knew either. Same thing with Danni's father."

"Joan?" Sophia quirked a curious eyebrow.

He nodded. "My mother."

"You call her Joan?"

His eyes narrowed. "She's lucky I'm so nice."

And so started the story of his troubled past.

CHAPTER 24

Reed's hard tone as he mentioned Joan Walker caused Sophia to jerk back in surprise. She'd never known him to be hateful. But then the reality behind his scathing comment made her shiver. He despised his mother. What kind of nightmare did a person have to live through to loathe his own mother?

She swallowed. "I'm not going to like this story, am I?"

He didn't answer. But he didn't need to. "I don't think she started out as a bad mom. Some of my earliest memories of her were when she was pregnant with Danni."

"How old were you then?"

"Seven." He shrugged. "I remember Joan didn't want the baby. She was very upset about it. She had a miserable pregnancy and snapped at me a lot. I was surprised by her behavior. It actually hurt my feelings, which makes me think she wasn't always so awful. Don't you think?" He glanced at Sophia.

Not sure how to answer, Sophia merely nodded. "I guess."

Reed nodded too. "I think she was at least halfway decent up to that point." It seemed like he needed to believe that statement for his own peace of mind.

Sophia remained stoically quiet, her gut clenching.

"After Danni was born, though, everything changed. Joan changed. I don't know if it was Postpartum depression or what. But she didn't want to be a mother, and she let us know it every chance she got. I'm not sure why she kept us, why she didn't get an abortion or give us up for adoption. But I know she received extra money from the government for having children, so maybe that was it."

"What about Social Services?" Sophia asked. "Why didn't they come and…" She trailed off at Reed's amused look.

"They don't just go knocking on every door, seeing if there are any neglected kids inside."

Sophia sent him a reproachful look. "Well, I know that. It's just…why didn't any neighbor call her in or—"

She stopped again when Reed laughed harshly. "We didn't exactly live in a neighborhood where there were a lot of concerned citizens worried about our welfare. I know the crack dealer down the hall certainly wasn't going to call any kind of law enforcement into the building."

Sophia gaped at him. She never would've guessed that someone as well-groomed, polite-mannered, and self-controlled as Reed Walker had grown up in that kind of environment.

"She had a lot of boyfriends," Reed said, ready to continue. "Joan was very popular with the guys. But she never kept them long. A couple moved in with us over the years, but no one stayed over a month or two. There was this one, he actually broke up with her because of the way she treated Danni and me."

He was quiet a moment. Thoughtful. "I remember being mad at Joan after he left. I liked him, though for the life of me, I can't remember his name. They had this yelling match one night in her bedroom. We could hear everything they said. He told her she disgusted him, and she wasn't even a real woman because she didn't take care of her own children. Then there was this slapping sound. A second later, he stormed out of the bedroom with a bright red mark on his face.

"He stopped when he saw me. After pulling out his wallet, he gave me all the cash he had on him. He said, 'Don't let your mother have any of this.'" Reed looked rather satisfied when he glanced at Sophia. "I didn't either. I didn't let her find any of it." He sighed, refreshed. "Danni and I ate good that month."

A ball formed in Sophia's throat. She wanted to cry for the boy he described.

His eyes darkened, and his gaze became shuttered. He wasn't looking at her now, but at a spot on the wall, or maybe through the wall into the past.

"Not all of her men were so kind."

Sophia shuddered. Suddenly, she didn't want to hear any more. She wanted to tell Reed he didn't have to talk. She didn't want to know—

"His name was Francis Moorehouse." Chilled, Sophia clamped her hands tightly together. She didn't like the dull look in Reed's gaze, the toneless way he added, "But he's dead now." He glanced at her briefly, not even focusing on her. "I went to his funeral and looked into the coffin at his face to make sure." He nodded reassuringly. "He is definitely dead."

Sophia had a feeling she should be grateful Francis Moorehouse was definitely dead. "How…" she started to ask but had to pause and clear her throat when her voice went hoarse. "How did he die?"

Reed shrugged. "Some kind of fight when he was in jail. I'm not sure. I just know he was incarcerated and a fellow inmate killed him during a dispute."

Sophia nodded, letting him continue.

"He wasn't with Joan very long. They had a very…violent relationship. The police came once to break them up. Joan didn't put up with it for long. She kicked him out and told Danni and me to never let him in the house again."

Reed's chin trembled. "But he got in anyway."

He stopped talking and frowned as if trying desperately to stop the shuddering in his jaw. He even wiped a hand over his lower face. Sophia had to look away and bite down hard on her bottom lip. Lord, she didn't want to cry. She didn't even know what Francis Moorehouse had done yet. But it had obviously scarred Reed for life.

"I was twelve years old. Danni was five. God, she was only *five*," he whispered in a tortured voice.

Sophia lifted a hand to her mouth, already guessing the worst.

"He came pounding on the door one day, shouting for Joan." He cleared his throat and wiped his hand over his face. "I was in the kitchen, trying to find something to eat. All we had were stale crackers and molding butter."

"Where was your mom?" Sophia whispered. *Where the hell was Joan?*

He shrugged. "I don't know. She'd gotten some new boyfriend. I hadn't seen her for a few days."

"Oh my God. Weren't you worried she was never going to come back?"

"No. I mean, she always came back...eventually."

"She left more than *once?*" Sophia gaped. "For days?"

He looked at her. His eyes answered, *Yes, all the time.*

Her mouth fell open and she could only stare. She wanted to find Joan Walker and strangle the life out of her.

"I told Danni to hide in the hall closet." Reed went back to staring at the wall with a fixed and blank stare. "By the way he was hammering on the door, I worried he'd break in. Which he did..." He shook his head as if he wasn't quite clear about what happened next. After sixteen years, the facts were no doubt distorted in his memory. "Just as we heard the door splinter in the living room, I shoved Danni into the closet and slammed the door. A second later, he barreled around the corner, looking capable of murder."

Reed's entire body shuddered. Sophia found herself shivering as well. She rubbed at her prickling arms.

"He wanted to know where Joan was..." He paused, scowling as if deep in thought, trying to recall every little detail.

"I lied. I told him she'd taken Danni somewhere. I can't

even remember what I said, that they were shopping or something. He let out a ripe curse and shoved me aside, charging back to Joan's room to make sure she was really gone. From that point on, he trashed the place, taking whatever he wanted. I didn't fight him. I knew I'd lose if I tried. But then he found my stash of cash I'd been saving under my mattress. I wasn't sure how we'd pay the rent if he took that money, so I charged him, slamming my fist right in his gut."

Sophia grinned, silently cheering for the twelve-year-old Reed.

"When he caught me," Reed said, a stony expression on his face. "He wrenched my arm back until I cried out and then...then he threw me against the wall."

Sophia winced.

"It must've knocked me out because the next thing I remember...I was on my stomach with my face in the carpet. My clothes were strewn across the floor of the hall, and he was on top of me. Inside me."

"*What?*" Sophia nearly yelled. Never in a million years had she expected this twist in the story.

Reed stopped talking; Sophia didn't think she could have taken it if he'd kept going. She shook her head at his words, desperate to deny them. She didn't even realize she'd started crying until she reached up to wipe the tears off her face.

"You'd think with a mother like I had," he croaked in a choppy voice, "I'd know all about sex by then. I mean, yeah, I knew what it was. I knew the basics of how it happened, but I didn't—I never thought an adult was capable to doing it to a... I had no idea it could happen to a *boy*."

"Oh God, Reed." Sophia cupped both hands over her face. "No."

He wasn't even fazed by her sympathetic moan. He stared vacantly ahead, trapped in the memories.

"No," Sophia repeated. She shook her head frantically. "No, no, *no!*" She surged from her seat and hurled herself at him, wrapping her arms around his legs and openly sobbing against his knees.

He patted her head and ran his hand comfortingly over her hair.

"But it was okay," he assured. "It was okay. Danni was safe in the closet. I just kept repeating that through my head. He's away from Danni. He's away from Danni. He's not doing this to Danni."

Sophia whimpered and clung more tightly. She couldn't believe this. Not Reed. Not her beautiful, strong Reed.

"I just...I don't think I would've been able to handle it if he'd done that to Danni." He busied his hands by continuing to stroke her hair. "That was all I could think at first. At least it wasn't Danni. But then I looked over and saw her peeking out the closet, her eyes wide and frightened, and I got so worried that he'd see her and go after her next."

"Oh, Reed." Sophia pressed her cheek to his knee, soaking his pant leg with her tears. He needed to stop. He had to stop talking. She couldn't listen to any more.

But he kept going.

"After that, I could feel the pain. I mean, I don't remember it hurting before then. But when I thought she was going to be next, it suddenly hurt like...like nothing has ever hurt before or since. I managed to wave at her until she ducked back into the closet and shut the door. Then I screamed and I screamed until he put his hand over my mouth, cutting off my air."

He stopped, reliving the moment in his head for a while. Sophia felt drained during the short repose. Then Reed started in again.

"When he was done, he stood up and stared down at me for a while. I was so scared, and I don't know why. There was nothing worse he could've done to me. But I was too scared to look up at him. Finally, he said. 'Hmm. I never had a boy before. Not too bad, kid.' And he turned away.

"He finished ransacking the house, taking the rent money and stealing anything he could carry. Danni hurried from the closet and crawled to me while he was in another room. She had a blanket and covered me with it. Then she crawled under with me where we both hid until he left."

He grinned down at Sophia and then bent to lovingly nuzzle his face against her hair. "Afraid she was still in danger, I started to cry. I put my body on top of hers, hoping he didn't find her with me. He laughed when he saw the blanket. He kicked the sheet…caught me right in the side of the knee and said something like, 'Think I don't know you're under there, you little shit?' He thought it was extremely funny. But…" Reed shook his head, looking helpless. "I didn't know what else to do."

"You did good," Sophia told him, stroking his face and running her fingers over every wonderful feature. "You protected your sister. You did amazing."

He caught her gaze. "She's what kept me alive. I wouldn't have made it without her. I would've killed myself, I was so ashamed. Mortified. Disgusted. But Danni needed me. So I picked myself up and I carried her to the bathroom. I made us a bath and we sat in it together for probably an hour. When I drained the water, it was pink with blood."

Setting a hand over her mouth, Sophia thought she might be sick.

"After watching everything, Danni went catatonic. I pretty much had to function for her. I fed her and clothed her. She would just limply sit there, staring straight ahead. She didn't talk again for three weeks. Then one day, I woke up with her standing by my bed and staring at me. She told me she was hungry."

He shrugged. "After that, she was the same old Danni again. It was like nothing had ever happened. I thought she'd blocked it and didn't even remember. We never talked about it, and she never made one comment in reference to it. The subject was never broached again…not until the other day."

"What did your mom do when did she finally returned home?"

"She came home the next evening. She was mad that everything was gone. She yelled at me for letting him into the apartment."

Sophia gasped in outrage. "And she didn't even care that

he'd——"

"I didn't tell her," Reed said. "I couldn't."

"But she had to know that something was wrong. She had to sense——"

"Joan wasn't a real motherly individual."

"But she didn't notice *anything* wrong?"

"She asked me what was wrong with Danni. I think I said she was sick or something. I don't really remember. Those weeks directly after it were kind of a blur."

Sophia nodded, understanding. "How could you stay there? Why didn't you get help or——"

"Because of Danni," he cut in. "I went to school with this one kid. He had four other siblings. When they were taken away from his parents, they were all split up. None of them got to stay together." Reed shook his head emphatically. "There was no way I was going to let someone take Danni away from me. No way. She was my foundation, what kept me going."

"Oh, Reed." She sighed and rested her head on his shoulder as she stroked his jaw.

He caught her hand. Rubbing his thumb over the back of her palm, he moved so that their eyes could meet.

"I thought I was over this," he told her. "I thought...I don't know. I thought I'd pushed it so far down it could never come back up. But when Danni was attacked——" He paused to close his eyes and rub his cheek against her hand. "I can't believe it happened to her too. I feel like I failed her."

"No——" Sophia started, but he kept talking.

"All the nightmares came rushing back. I even started hating the dark again. And that makes no sense to me. It happened in broad daylight. But then, I guess, I dreamed about it afterward, reliving it a thousand times in my sleep. It always came back to haunt me in the dark. So I hated the dark."

He looked at her and smiled softly. "You helped me with that, though. I can stand the dark now because you gave me a new memory to replace old horrors."

He paused and licked his dry lips nervously. "I guess what I'm trying to say is...you heal me, Sophia. When I'm with you, everything is good and pure. You're a light in the dark. And I never wanted this to touch you or—"

"Shh." A fresh wave of tears spilled down her cheeks as she rose up and cupped his face. "Reed…"

He closed his eyes. "He made me dirty, Sophia. I'll never be good enough for you. I'll never—"

"Yes, you will," she assured. "You already are." A part of her wanted to laugh about the irony. All this time, she'd thought he was too good for her, and here, he'd presumed the same thing. "You are everything I have ever wanted in a man, Reed Walker."

He let out a relieved breath before he crushed his mouth to hers. "Sophia," he said, holding her close. His hands moved over her back. Happiness consumed her. "Remember when you told me not to tell you if I had a rough upbringing?"

She closed her eyes and smiled. "I remember I told you I'd probably fall in love with you on the spot if you did."

"But later you said you were through with men who had baggage and nasty secrets."

Wincing, she admitted, "I did claim that, didn't I?"

"Yeah, you did. And I can't help but wonder which statement was true."

Her smile was full of love as she answered, "Well, the first one, of course."

He pressed his forehead to hers. "If you were looking for a man with a painful past, then you found one."

Sophia was rather smug when she answered, "I knew I would. Does this mean I get to keep you?"

Reed stroked her face. "Only until forever."

EPILOGUE

When the wedding march started, Reed paused his pacing in the outer vestibule and turned toward the closed double doors that led into the sanctuary of the church. His stomach twitched with nervous anxiety.

It was time.

He pivoted back around, looking for the bride, but something snagged his pant leg, catching him off-guard. Glancing down to find five little fingers clamped around the polyester fabric of his trousers and a girl with his grey eyes and Sophia's strawberry blond curls staring up at him, he stopped in his tracks.

"Daddy, I can't find my flowers."

He picked up the three-year-old, the gossamer layers of her dress billowing over the black sleeve of his tux jacket, and scanned the atrium before spotting a wicker basket lying abandoned on its side under a nearby folding chair.

"Here they are." He strode to the basket and knelt down, still holding his daughter with one arm. After straightening the basket, he scooped up the pink rose petals that had spilled onto the red carpet and dropped them back into their container.

"Thank you, Daddy," the girl said as he set her back on her

feet and handed the basket over. Before he could push back to a stand, she leaned forward and smacked a grateful kiss to his clean-shaven jaw.

Love, powerful and all-consuming, slammed hard against the inside wall of his chest. Sometimes he still found it hard to believe this beautiful little human was his flesh and blood, and even more difficult to believe her mother was the one woman he couldn't live without.

"You're welcome," he murmured. Smiling, he smoothed his hand over Alyssa's hair, then tidied her white skirt that had become bunched in the back from where she'd been sitting on his arm.

"Now," he said, straightening to his full height and taking her hand. "I think we need to find your Aunt Danni and get this wedding started."

"I saw her with Momma, fixing something in Aunt Danni's hair," Alyssa reported, trotting along beside him as he frowned and moved toward a door that led into a side room, where he assumed his sister had been waiting for her big entrance down the aisle. But when he nudged the door open, Danni was not inside.

Behind him, a voice said, "Reed?"

He spun around, and the breath caught in his chest.

She was even more beautiful than the first day he'd started working at Kendrick Advertising and seen her walking down the hallway between cubicles.

Standing in the doorway to the bathroom, his wife seemed to glow with the light behind her shining through her red hair and around her pale pink matron of honor dress.

"Well, hello, Mrs. Walker." His voice went husky and suggestive.

She grinned, her eyes glittering with the same adoration he felt. "Hello, yourself," she returned. She moved toward him, practically floating with her graceful stroll. Clutching the lapels of his jacket, she tugged him an inch closer and pressed her warm mouth to his. He sank toward her and inhaled her love.

"Momma, you look so pretty," Alyssa exclaimed.

Sophia laughed against Reed's mouth before she looked down. "Not as pretty as you though," she said, tweaking her daughter's nose.

As the two females beamed at each other, a third entered the room, exiting the bathroom and smoothing down the skirt of her pure-white dress.

"Oh, my," Reed said, catching sight of his sister for the first time today. He'd spent the last few hours at Nic's side, trying to calm his friend's fried nerves before the big I do's and hadn't had a chance to check on his three girls or see how Danni looked in her dress.

She was a vision.

"Calhoun's eyes are going to pop out of their sockets when he sees you."

Grin stretching from ear to ear, Danni leapt toward him and hugged him around the neck. "Reed," she squealed. "I'm so happy. I can't believe today is already here."

"You better be happy," he said as he pulled back. "Or that groom of yours and I are going to have words."

At that moment, one of the double doors crept open and the wedding coordinator poked her head into the vestibule. "The groom's parents and grandparents are seated. It's time for the flower girl."

Alyssa flew forward. "That's me, that's me!"

Just as Reed was thinking how fast Alyssa had grown up into such a responsible young lady, Sophia took his hand. "Just look at her. I've never seen such an eager flower girl."

As Alyssa disappeared into the sanctuary, the coordinator waved Sophia forward. "Matron of honor," she called.

Sophia squeezed Reed's fingers, then reached over and kissed Danni's cheek before she disappeared as well, leaving the bride alone with her big brother.

"You look lovely," Reed said, taking her cold fingers and setting them in place at the crook of his elbow.

Her eyes glittered with tears. "Thank you. I *feel* lovely."

Together they turned toward the closed doors. A spark of disappointment filled him when he realized he wouldn't been able to see Alyssa dropping her flowers. She's been so excited about her job, she'd practiced at least fifty times at the rehearsal before Sophia stopped her and told her she had it down perfectly.

He also wished he could be at Nic's side, helping his friend through one of the most nerve-wracking moments of his life. Reed remembered how he had kept holding his breath when he'd been standing at the altar, waiting to see Sophia in her wedding dress. Nic had been there, quietly leaning toward him and murmuring, "Breathe, man, just breathe."

Jesus, he hoped Calhoun remembered to breathe.

Pulling double duty as the best man and pseudo father of the bride had its downside. But it also had its perks. He felt honored to be the one standing with Danni, waiting to give his sister away to his best friend.

He leaned toward her and grinned. "I never did sit you down to have the pre-wedding talk, did I?"

Danni rolled her eyes and blushed. "Reed, I know how sex works."

His smile dimmed. He'd only been trying to lighten the mood and keep her happy, but at the mention of that word, a small part of his brain flittered and stalled. "Yeah, but you learned about it all wrong."

Her eyes were huge and grey as she lifted her face and looked at him. He swallowed, wishing he hadn't brought that up. But she smiled, soft and loving. Her fingers squeezed reassuringly around his arm. "Don't worry. Nic taught me the right way."

Just as Sophia had taught Reed the same. His throat felt dry and his eyes too moist. Covering her fingers, he grinned back. "How'd we find two people wonderful enough to show us a way out of the dark and into the light?"

She shrugged. "Just lucky, I guess."

Or blessed beyond measure.

Without warning, the coordinator flung open both doors. Everyone inside the church surged to their feet and shifted around to stare at them.

Getting with the program, Reed escorted his sister to her groom.

When he caught sight of Nic straining around the crowd to peek down the aisle, he rolled his eyes, but was secretly glad both his buddy and sister were going to be so happy together. Happiness made the world a better place.

Seeking his own source of contentment, he glanced toward the matron of honor. When he found her eyes already on him, his heart swelled with satisfaction. Next to Sophia, their daughter danced around the floor, pointing at Danni and declaring to everyone that her aunt was the bride. Chuckles filled the room, and a blushing Sophia quickly bent to hush her. But Reed couldn't drum up one ounce of embarrassment; too much pride and joy filled him.

THE END

ABOUT THE AUTHOR

Linda grew up on a dairy farm in the Midwest as the youngest of eight children. Now she lives in Kansas with her husband, daughter, and their nine cuckoo clocks. Her life's been blessed with lots of people to learn from and love. Writing's always been a major part her world, and she's so happy to finally share some of her stories with other romance lovers. Please visit her at her website

http://www.lindakage.com/

Kiss It Better